11-22-1963

New Evidence

A Novel

By

Roy Widing

11-22-1963
New Evidence

First Edition
ISBN 0615546234
Copyright 2011, Quality House
All rights reserved

11-22-1963.com

While fictional characters in this novel may bear resemblance to real people
in history, they are in fact complete inventions of the author's imagination.
No historical or otherwise real person appears in this book.

Why This Book?

President John F. Kennedy was murdered in Dallas, Texas on November 22, 1963. Most Americans still believe President Kennedy was slain as part of a conspiracy. Is the ability to definitively solve his murder forever gone? And how could anything possibly be changed about the events of 11-22-1963?

President Kennedy's murder cannot be reversed. Nor can we alter the wounding of Texas Governor John Connally as he rode with the president through Dealey Plaza. Also unchangeable is the killing of President Kennedy's alleged murderer, Lee Harvey Oswald, by nightclub owner Jack Ruby soon after President Kennedy's assassination. Nor can Jack Ruby's death while serving time in prison be undone. Given all these facts, why this book?

What *can* be changed about November 22, 1963 is more accurately determining those behind the president's death. The way to do this is stunning in its simplicity and earth-shaking in its effect. The answer to finally solving this crime, arguably the biggest mystery of the past century, is found in new evidence.

Why is new evidence important? Because half a dozen suspected parties are reported as having means, motive and opportunity to kill the president. New evidence can narrow the focus to those actually criminally involved.

Was Lee Harvey Oswald the lone gunman? Did he have help? Was there a government cover-up? Did the Mafia have a part in the killing? Were rogue members of the CIA, or the US military-industrial complex complicit in President Kennedy's death? Did the Russians or Cubans conspire? Was there a shot from the grassy knoll, or a second gunman inside the Texas Schoolbook Depository?

Given countless unanswered questions, new evidence can finally provide conclusive answers about who killed President John F. Kennedy. This book shows how yet-undiscovered information on the murder of President Kennedy may one day provide this new evidence.

But how could new evidence be found? Fresh evidence on President Kennedy's assassination as described in **11-22-1963** has already surfaced and more continues to come out. As a result, additional new evidence on the crime appears likely. When it comes to solving this most vexing of high profile mysteries, we may indeed find that truth is stranger than any novel.

Table of Contents

<u>Chapter I</u>

A Mystery Awakened

For there is nothing covered, that shall not be revealed;
neither hid, that shall not be known. Luke 12:2

Hands jingling coins in his pocket, real estate agent Ron Winston's anxiety about a potential deal-killing home inspection was obvious. "Anything interesting up there?"

"Clean as a whistle. Attic's dry; no leaks. Plenty of insulation, though. From here, looks like an old box is wedged in the far corner."

"A box? The seller's real estate agent said her clients took everything with them when they moved out. Take a look at whatever's left up there. Anything remaining could be up for grabs."

The life of a real estate agent is strange. Because every day is different, it's impossible to know what might happen next. Sometimes it's a big sale. At other times it's an unusual home inspection. But only the most unusual home inspection reveals a movie camera with undeveloped footage of an unsolved presidential assassination.

The house wasn't fancy by Dallas standards and real estate agent Winston's homebuyers were particularly picky. So to ensure the property was worth touring, he'd previewed the place alone a few days earlier. As

Winston first retrieved house keys from the multiple listing lockbox hanging on the front door, something told him his buyers would be making an offer on this one. Call it a hunch, but the place had charm. Passing through the main entrance on his maiden tour, Winston detected a hint of mothballs and smiled.

Good, he thought. *If the sellers were as concerned about the house as their clothes, this place should be in decent condition.*

A veteran of good markets and bad, Winston knew the real estate business. The next day he tugged his multiple listing printout from a battered, coffee-stained file folder. After Winston opened the door for his buyers with a bow and flourish, he calmly read the basics.

"On the market for 5 days. 3,600 square feet...three bedrooms, two full baths, one of them 'super-adequate.' That's real estate lingo for extra large, folks. There's also a fireplace on the main floor. The house is decades old, but appears well-maintained."

Several moments of quiet ensued, followed by the kind of enthusiastic client response salespeople love to hear: "Oh look, John...hardwood floors!"

In addition to his tall, lanky frame, one other trait set Ron Winston apart from the faceless pack of real estate agents. He simply refused to use the hard sell, disliking any association with pushy sales types. Particularly revolting to Winston were those using the infamous "car dealer con," a technique made famous by auto salesmen throwing prospective buyers' keys on a showroom roof to keep them from leaving. Besides,

Winston was more than a real estate agent. He held membership in several trade organizations that actually had ethical codes.

From his first days in real estate, Winston saw himself as a professional. Sure, he was a salesman and wanted a deal. Sometimes he even had to fight that side of himself a bit. But his work was guided by one simple philosophy he frequently explained to rookie real estate agents. "Treat people the way you want to be treated. It's a relationship you're building." "Besides," he'd invariably add, "Why use a bazooka when a pea-shooter will do?"

During his early years in business, Winston noticed the most successful real estate agents had plenty of repeat customers. He also learned it took ten times the effort to get a new customer as it did to retain an existing one. It made perfect sense to stay in touch with previous clients and treat them well. "That's why the real estate salesperson drop out rate is 80% in the first two years alone," Winston once heard in a sales seminar, along with the adage "Plan your work and work your plan." Now with plenty of referrals after more than twenty years in the trenches, Winston was reaping the benefits of his well-planned strategy.

Winston first met current buyer clients John and Carol Westmoreland at an open house weeks earlier. With great credit and a decent down payment, they were the kind of buyers any real estate agent could appreciate. Most helpful to Winston, they knew what they wanted. Guesswork removed, finding their next home should be simple, he reasoned. Strolling the grounds, Winston continued to scribble notes for their home purchase while his buyers continued to emit obvious buying signals. Sure enough, by the time the Westmoreland's saw the workshop, Winston's special *Montblanc* "offer pen" was out. Winston knew they wanted the place. But like most cautious house-hunters, they still sought approval.

"Can we afford it, Ron?"

Having already spoken with his favorite lender, it was easy for Winston to tell his homebuyers what they wanted to hear. In his most assuring voice, he calmly responded. "Interest rates have only gone down since I last crunched the numbers. You shouldn't have any trouble." Winston grinned. "Besides, do you think I'd show you something you couldn't buy?"

With this blessing, they all re-entered the house. Winston saw John and Carol admire the home's oak floors accented in black walnut inlay. *These clients act like they're kids again*, he marveled, still sensing they hoped for some kind of cosmic confirmation sign. Looking up, polished brass fixtures hung gracefully from the twelve foot ceiling. *Not a cobweb in sight*, Winston thought thankfully. He always seemed to get buyers terrified of spiders. The large kitchen opened up to a living room so large it literally echoed as the three of them passed through toward a massive brick fireplace.

They all trooped outside again to view the backyard. Just off the kitchen in back, the cobblestone patio led to a manicured lawn. At half an acre, the lot was larger than it appeared from the street. Always several steps ahead, Winston pondered silently: *I wonder what kind of condition they'll have it in if they decide to trade up in a few years?*

Winston rambled back toward the house to give his buyers some breathing room. After an appropriate wait, he returned outside. They were gone. Winston walked back inside on the hunt for his customers and climbed the staircase. Peering into a master bathroom, he murmured: "That jetted-tub is big enough for six people—practically a swimming pool."

Still searching for his buyers, Winston headed downstairs. He caught up with Carol as she admired the roomy kitchen.

"This is so much bigger than our old place," she smiled as her voice echoed.

We're moving in the right direction, thought Winston as he looked at his clients. "One of the advantages to buying a vacant home like this, Carol and John, is that you can move in on the day of closing, so there's no delay with the possession date."

Always mindful to avoid pressuring his clients, Winston waited for his buyers to show a few more obvious buying signals. Before long, Winston's home purchase documents were conspicuously positioned on the gleaming white tile counter for their John and Jane Hancock. John and Carol had initially hoped to haggle, but really wanted the home. In less than twenty minutes, their full price offer was signed.

As the three were on their way out the main entry, Winston mentally calculated his commission. Half an hour later, he stopped at his office, e-mailed the offer to the listing real estate agent and waited. And waited. After one full day and two nervous phone calls from his buyer clients, Winston received a return call from the seller's agent.

"Ron, I presented your offer to my clients."

"How'd it go, Sheila?"

"Fine…accepted as written. But my people were wondering if we could close sooner. They've already signed on their out-of-state purchase. The lender's letter for your buyers was so glowing, we figured they could wrap things up in three weeks instead of five."

"Better be a clean inspection, then," Winston quipped. And that's what had him holding his breath three days later as the house inspector descended the ladder with a yellowed, decaying box in his beefy hand.

"I opened the box up. It's a movie camera, alright…says Bell & Howell on it. My kid brother had one of these. Got his at a flea market. They were big back in the day. I wonder if it still works?"

Winston lifted the camera box and was impressed by its heft. "I'll call the listing agent and make sure the sellers don't want it."

"It was so far back there, it would have been easy to miss. Wedged between drywall and insulation. But a chipmunk or mouse must've torn into the side. The only reason I found it is because I could see the paper trail from where I was crouching."

"How'd the rest of the house look?"

"The owners took care of this place. Aside from a little dry rot on the main floor and needing a rodent trap in the attic, it looks pretty darn good for a home of this age."

Unsure if the old camera was simply a worthless relic, Winston tossed it in the back seat of his car. *Funny,* he thought as he sat behind his steering wheel on the drive home. *As a 4-H club reporter, little Ronnie Winston always wanted his own movie camera. Now decades later, it looks like maybe I finally got my wish.*

Later that evening, Winston picked up the phone and dialed. "Hi Sheila—Ron at Lone Star Realty. You've been hard to reach!"

"Sorry, Ron. My Mom is here from out of town. How did the inspection go?"

"Pretty clean. A little dry rot in the downstairs bathroom, but it shouldn't delay closing."

"Great. My people are so focused on their next house, they'll do what it takes to get repairs done on time. I'll get started on bids. Did the inspector find any termites or carpenter ants?"

"Just a chipmunk in the attic and a beat up old camera. Think they want it?"

"No, the sellers are long gone. They said anything else could be thrown out."

"Fine, Sheila. Please call me once the dry rot bids are in."

"Will do. Thanks, Ron."

No. Thank you, Winston thought as he dialed his friend Gene.

"Plano Pawn."

"Hey Gene, it's Ron Winston."

"Ron. How goes it, my real estate friend? Selling an estate property, are we?"

"Not this time—I've got a movie camera for you to look at."

"What kind is it?"

"A Bell & Howell."

"What makes you think I'm interested?"

"You buy cameras, right?"

"Does it work?"

"I don't know. Look...I may want to keep it, anyway. I'm just curious about what it might be worth."

"If it doesn't work, I've got no use for it. If it does, maybe I can find a sucker, part it out...or sell it to someone who still thinks it's the 20th century."

"What do you mean?"

"Ron, if you had a still camera, it'd be different. I sell plenty of quality old still film cameras. Rollei, Hasselblad, the whole shot. But demand for old movie cameras is virtually dead. They're history...literally."

A salesman himself, Winston took a deep breath. "Are you softening me up for a lowball appraisal?"

"Not at all. It's about the technology. These days, movie camera buyers have gone digital. They're easy and instant, with no film to develop. For whatever reason, still photographers remain purists when it comes to using film...they actually seem to *prefer* it. Something about a 'warmer' look. So the market for old still cameras is soft, but at least steady. Not old movie cameras. You need a favor? I'll see what I can do. But if you bring it in here, make sure it works."

"It looks like it's in good shape...what do they go for now in good condition?"

"Honestly?"

"Honestly."

"Not much."

"I'll think about it. Thanks."

As the two men hung up, Gene mumbled unapologetically at his phone. "I have to make a living. Everybody tries to unload their junk on me. They think I'm running a flea market."

Fingers drumming the oak desk in his real estate office a few days later, Ron Winston had better things to do than think about a virtually-worthless camera. But old dreams die hard. Long after he'd abandoned the youthful wish of owning a movie camera, the thought still intrigued him. Sure, he already had plenty of cameras, including one he received on his eighth birthday. And there was the Nikon 35mm he got as a college graduation present. But he still liked the idea of making his own movies. And free was a *very* good price.

Winston lobbied himself to keep the camera. "Gene's probably right. It isn't worth much, anyway. Oh well, I got it for free. Might as well find out if it works."

Reaching across his desk for the rectangular camera box, Winston flipped open the faded crumbling cover and felt inside. Lifting it out, the silver camera had the look of a Cyclops and the heft of a small tire jack. He looked on the side of the machine, then slowly cranked half a dozen times on what appeared to be a windup mechanism. Peeking through the viewfinder, he swiveled in his chair and looked out the window behind him. Pretending to film an approaching car, Winston saw the passing vehicle in his viewfinder and uttered "If this camera could talk."

Winston's index finger moved along the silver camera's side starting button and slowly pushed it down. A gentle "Whirrrrrrr" emanated from the long-silent machine.

"Hey! It still works!" Bolting upright from his desk, Winston carefully laid the camera down. Staring at it, he rubbed his chin and said: "If the gears are still working, what about film?" Winston had destroyed plenty of otherwise good photographs in his youth by opening cameras in broad daylight, unsure if they were loaded with film. He picked up the device and gently placed it back in the box. Summoning his laptop, online he found a nearby firm billed as "Your 8mm Specialists." "Bingo," he whispered. It was a ten minute drive.

Winston entered Cowboy Camera not to the jingle jangle of spurs, but the high pitched tinkle of a door bell. At the store entrance, a sun-bleached film display with a thick coat of dust greeted him. Winston surmised the store had been around a long time. But if the digital age had arrived, no one told the man behind the register in this sleepy Dallas suburb. Straight out of nerd central casting, he wore a white shirt, thin tie, pocket protector and an eager grin. Winston lifted the movie camera out of its disintegrating box.

"Can you tell me if there's any film in here to develop?

"You don't know?"

"It was a gift. But if there isn't any in there, I'll need a few rolls."

"Let me check it out in the darkroom first. I know we have that film in stock."

The clerk returned several minutes later.

"It's loaded, alright. But the film looks to be about half used up. Do you want it developed?"

"Naw, thanks. I'll bring it in when I'm done with the roll that's in there now. But I will take a few more rolls of film. I've got a vacation planned.

Chapter II

Government Work

The wedding rehearsal banquet at an upscale Dallas steak house was about to begin. Wayne Schaefer grabbed his spoon, clanged his wine glass and cleared his throat.

"I propose a toast...To Audrey. May my niece's marriage to Steve be long and filled with love...and rugrats galore."

With echoes of laughter and champagne glasses raised around the room, two dozen diners erupted in unison, chanting hearty approval: "To Audrey."

Except for flecks of grey at his temples, Wayne Schaefer didn't look 64. Husky and ruggedly handsome, in college he'd been a dead ringer for one especially famous swashbuckling movie actor of old Hollywood. Despite his age, Schaefer remained dashing and still carried his roguish swagger.

Several key abilities made Wayne Schaefer exceptionally well-suited for his role as a CIA officer. A devoted poker player, Schaefer could also be hard to read. Given his hardscrabble childhood, he had the knack to relate with people from all walks of life with his affable nature. But what made Schaefer deadly effective was his disarming, self-deprecating sense of humor. If someone didn't care for him, Schaefer could still make them laugh...even if it meant they were laughing at him. From that point, it was just a matter of time before he had them. When it came to human chemistry, Wayne Schaefer was a chemist par excellence.

Wayne Schaefer was attending this wedding rehearsal dinner out of sincere affection for both his sister and niece. With initial festivities out of the way and the main course begun, the crowd quieted to a buzz. Now in a relaxed mood with several Moscow Mules under his belt, Schaefer stirred with the swizzle stick in his drink before voicing his curiosity to the young man seated nearby. "Hey Skip…how's your old man doing? I haven't seen him in too long."

The pasty-faced man sharing a corner of the table spoke his lines unconvincingly, as if memorized.

"He's retired, Mr. Schaefer. I talk to him a few times a month. Dad's enjoying his freedom. When he's not golfing he's fishing. I'm a little jealous."

Schaefer discreetly lowered his voice and looked at the younger man eye-to-eye. "Skip. This may be none of my business, but I remember the plans your Dad had for you. Honestly…how does he feel about you working in a camera shop at what, 40?"

Skip Hollister cleared his throat self-consciously. "Thirty eight, Mr. Schaefer. And I like my job just fine."

Hollister straightened up in his chair, elbows firmly planted on the table. "Photography is my career. It pays my bills and the work is steady. Besides, I like it and I'm good at it. That's more than a lot of people can say."

A teddy bear of a man, Schaefer glanced at Skip Hollister in a fatherly manner. "Skip, you know my son Rich. He's your age and got on with the agency three years ago. He loves it, just like I knew he would. And while most of the great assignments come later, it's like anything else; you work your way up. So he's thinking long term and you could, too. The only reason I'm mentioning it is because I talked with Rich the other day and he said they're in recruiting mode right now. Skip, it's never too late to shift career gears."

The younger man responded quietly, but with modulated tension in his voice. "I appreciate the suggestion, Mr. Schaefer, I really do. But I've had a long time to consider what kind of job I want. No offense, but what you think is a great job doesn't work for me. I had the late night pep-talks from my Dad, too. But you know what I'm left with? All those lost birthdays and holidays with Dad off in some hostile, faraway country. The worst part was never knowing when, or even if, he'd walk back through our doorway. And it wasn't like we could just call him whenever we wanted."

"I understand, believe me," Schaefer nodded knowingly, further lowering his voice to almost a whisper. "Sure it gets hairy at times. I missed my share of family gatherings, staked out in some God-forsaken third world country. I realize it isn't for everybody and seniority doesn't always count for much. For example, as of last year I'm technically on stand-by…unless things really heat up, anyway. Yet when it hits the fan, that's when they decide experience counts and pull us old guys off the shelf. But I'm still an intel wonk at heart and I know potential. Skip, you have potential and believe me, you *can* work your way up. Plus these days, it isn't all 'out of country' stuff, like what your Dad and I put up with. Since 9/11, so much has changed."

Schaefer plunged a fist into his coat pocket, fished out a pen and scribbled on the napkin between them. "Look. Here's Rich's number…he's the one to talk to. These days, he knows a lot more about the new policies and opportunities than I do. Think it over. If you change your mind, or just want to know the straight scoop, give him a call. With your degree and photographic background, you'd fit right in. At great pay, too. And benefits? Man. But even if you don't want to talk careers, I know Rich would like to reminisce about your days trolling on the lake."

Schaefer gave the younger man a grin like they'd both just caught lunkers. "Think about it?"

Skip Hollister shrugged his shoulders. "Sure, Mr. Schaefer. If I change my mind, I'll let you know. And I appreciate the encouragement, I really do. But just to be straight with you, please don't get your hopes up."

"No problem, Skip," Schaefer responded. "Just remember; I'm here for you. You've been like a nephew to me. Whatever you decide."

Several days later, a familiar tinkling doorbell heralded Ron Winston's return to Cowboy Camera.

21

"Can I help you?"

"I'm here to pick up some film for Winston."

Beginning his search in the bins behind him, Skip Hollister seemed distracted. "First name?"

"Ron."

"What kind of film?"

"Eight millimeter. I dropped off several rolls a few weeks ago."

Turning to a tray of metallic silver film rolls resembling obese drink coasters, Hollister exclaimed in a descending tone: "Eight millimeter rolls for Winston..."

Several moments later, he exclaimed: "Oh, here they are." Holding the developed film containers in both hands, Hollister walked over to the cash register. Ringing up the order, he looked up at Winston.

"I happened to develop these myself and was wondering...is one of them some kind of an indie film?"

"What do you mean?"

"For quality control, I spot-check everything to adjust for under or over-exposed film. As I remember, one roll had an 'edgy' feel to it...grainy and realistic. Authentic looking...like some of Oliver Stone's work. I'm personally not much into that gritty, dark 'noir' stuff; too strong for me. The genre's popular, though. I hear the French like it, anyway. Very sophisticated."

Puzzled, but too tired to discuss the minutiae of modern film technique, Winston had heard enough.

"Right. I guess taste determines art. By the way, do you rent 8mm film projectors?"

"$30 a week."

"I'll take one of them, too."

Handing Winston a pen, Hollister rattled off the shop's rental policy. "I'll need a photocopy of your driver's license and the late charge is $10 a day. Just fill in your address and phone number. I'll be right back."

Hollister walked to a tiny room behind the counter. A minute or two later, he returned with a rectangular box stenciled "8MM/Rental" on the side.

"How much do I owe you?"

Hollister punched the calculator before him.

"Let's see…$18.50 for developing, $30 for the projector rental and a deposit of $25. Your total is $73.50."

"I won't need it longer than a week. Here you go."

"And $6.50 is your change."

"Thanks."

Winston headed for the door.

"Thank you. Just make sure to turn off the projector lamp when you're not using it. The unit can get very hot and it shortens the bulb life."

"Sure thing."

With a tinkle of the doorbell, Winston lumbered across the lot to his car, one arm cradling the projector like a protective fullback. Something nagged at him as he tossed the white paper film sack on the front passenger seat and digested the conversation moments earlier. Winston began shaking his head.

"Edgy feel? Gritty dark 'noir' stuff? Either he was joking, or I've been pegged as some artiste type."

Happy to be off work, Winston pulled out of the parking lot. Minutes later he was heading home on Interstate 35 and ready to lay plans for the weekend ahead.

"Think I'll call Suze, set up the projector and relive our daytrip around Galveston Harbor. What a day that was. I wonder how my dolphin close-ups came out?"

Traffic to the Dallas suburbs slowed to a crawl, but 30 minutes later Winston was home. Pulling into the driveway of his two-level contemporary, Winston pressed the garage door opener and eased his late model Saab into the yawning structure. Passing through the kitchen, his cell phone alerted him to a voice message. Winston pressed the "listen" button. It was from his fiance', Suzanne.

"Hi Ron. My Mom just called. She needs help planning things for Dad's birthday. Do you mind if we get together tomorrow instead? I have the next three days off from work. Call me before you go to bed, okay? Love ya."

A single long beep at the end of the message put an exclamation point on Winston's now distinctively bachelor evening. He greeted the vacant Thursday night ahead with a sigh and walked over to the refrigerator. Pulling out a large blue and gold can of Foster's Lager saved for just such an occasion, Winston popped the metal top. He grabbed one of the perpetually chilled glasses from his freezer, angled the can and poured just the right amount of foam. "I'm tired, anyway," he exhaled, grabbing the TV remote. Twenty minutes later, the beer was gone.

"Awww, there's nothing on," Winston griped. "Why can't there be at least *one* decent night game on this week?"

Walking through the kitchen, Winston surveyed leftovers in the refrigerator and decided his late lunch had been enough for now. Hiking upstairs to change clothes, he spotted the bag of just-developed movie film on a table near the stairway. "Might as well keep it movie night," he told himself.

Winston loped upstairs, trance-like. Throwing his shirt on the butler's helper near the bed, he changed from slacks to his most comfortable worn chinos. Heading downstairs, Winston snatched the white paper bag. Standing beside the rented machine, he opened the box and carefully looped film through the projector's maze-like loading mechanism. Switching the machine on as he hit a wall switch, Winston yelled "Lights" and a blur danced before him. "Focus, too," he observed. Winston next pointed the one-eyed machine to an adjacent bare wall and adjusted the projector lens.

Turning to face the moving images, Winston didn't recognize the scenery. This film wasn't about him, or the trip he'd taken several months earlier. The movie showed a sunny day. It began with an extreme close up of a middle-aged man's face, followed by a dizzying spin of the camera. For a few moments, the image was of a young boy. As the film continued to roll, it became vaguely familiar. Less than a minute later, Winston recognized several now-old buildings in downtown Dallas.

One image of a building was instantly recognizable. He remembered parallel parking in front of it during his driver's education test as a teenager. Judging from the cars, clothing and black and white film, he pegged the time-frame as early 1960's. In seconds, Winston's eyes changed from tired to curious about what he was viewing.

The partially washed-out footage that followed revealed a distant approaching caravan with motorcycle escort. Flags fluttered on the hood of a looming limousine as if in slow motion. The event seemed eerily familiar, yet Winston still couldn't quite place it. As the figures in the vehicle grew larger he recognized the indisputably chiseled face of former Texas Governor John Connally seated in the car. As it hit Winston he gasped aloud: "This looks like…"

Moments later, he realized the film offered a very different perspective. This was indeed the president's motorcade through Dallas. But it wasn't moving on the screen in the familiar perspective like so many recycled TV documentaries. Instead, this was filmed from a different angle. He observed the long dark limo approach a tall building, then suddenly change direction. Transfixed by what he realized was about to occur, Winston felt numb.

A small flash appeared in the upper right hand corner of the screen. The motorcade turned as the camera continued to film where the car had been for several seconds, then raced to catch it back into view. A distinct spark from the ground appeared some distance from the president's car. The camera view moved to center on a white fence ahead and opposite from the presidential limousine. *This photographer was a real novice,* Winston thought as the film continued to roll. A puff of smoke appeared from above the distant fence. His stomach churned and he began to feel sick in witnessing the sudden movement inside the president's vehicle. As the film projector's "whir" continued, he noticed people pointing to a nearby hill. Pandemonium broke out in the plaza.

Still the film kept rolling. Parade vehicles sped off. People looked stunned. Some covered their mouths, others simply stood, dazed. Winston continued watching the movie as the view focused back on the fence. A policeman approached, then a hand covered the lens and everything went black. A moment later on the movie screen, Winston recognized the images as having been taken from his office desk, followed by film clips of his

Galveston Bay vacation. He reached over, switched off the projector and stared at the wall.

Like most Texans, Winston was familiar with President Kennedy's infamous Dallas visit on November 22, 1963. Then just four years old, he remembered nothing of the event itself. Yet as Thanksgiving approached every year since, the same decades-old story was rehashed on the news. It was a predictably observed Texas rite. And while solemn like Memorial Day, it was no longer as formal. But like the President himself, November 22nd came and passed, with candles lit each year in his memory. That it happened not in some backwater town, but in Dallas remained sobering to every Texan.

Hours later in his bed, Winston couldn't sleep. Each time his eyes wandered to the blue digital numbers on his dresser, he swore they hadn't changed. Now pushing his phone's speed-dial, he wondered aloud: "What did I witness?"

"Hello?" The young woman's voice was groggy.

"Suze, it's me."

"Ron…is something wrong?"

"I can't sleep."

"It's almost two in the morning. What's the matter?"

"You remember the movie camera I found?"

"You mean that antique you took on our trip?"

"Right. Well, I got the film back."

"How did it turn out?"

Winston gazed at his fiance's big brown eyes in the photo by his bed. "I'm not sure, but I think it could be evidence of a crime."

"Crime? What do you mean? You took movies of us."

"There was some old footage still in the camera. It looks like a film of President Kennedy when he was shot in Dallas."

"But Ron, that's not new. There's a movie of that already."

"This film looks different than anything I've seen before. Some of it's closer up, from a different angle and with different scenes."

"What are you going to do?"

"I don't know. That's why I'm calling you. I'm not sure."

"Shouldn't you call the police?"

"I was thinking of that."

"Well, let me know what you decide. I'll go with you if you need encouragement."

"Yeah. I just might need some. I feel better talking to you about it, though."

"You know you can call me anytime. Now that we're both awake, do you want me to come over and give you a massage?"

"I'd love it, but I know what I need to do."

"What's that?"

"Call my legal guy, first thing in the morning. Are we still on for getting together tomorrow night?"

"That sounds nice, Ron. We haven't had dinner out for a while and you can tell me what you find out about your movie."

"Dinner would be great. I'll pick you up at seven. By then, I should know what I'm dealing with here."

"Okay. But call me if you need to talk."

"I will. Love ya, Suze."

"Love you too, Ron. Bye."

At 6:30 the next morning, Winston awoke with the eerie feeling he'd survived a nightmare. But one glance at the projector in his living room convinced him it hadn't been just a bad dream. Clad in pajamas and not at all hungry, Winston padded to his computer and logged onto the Internet, typing "John Kennedy assassination" into a search engine. Up came hundreds of websites, each with its unique slant on the event.

As Winston scrolled through a few of them, one particular page caught his eye. Under "Frequently Asked Questions," he saw a sub-title: "Is the Zapruder film the only film of the assassination?" Winston literally shivered as he read the answer: "Yes and no. It is the only film known to exist showing most of the shooting. However, at least three photographers thought to have filmed part or all of the event remain unidentified and their films, if extant, remain unseen."

Later playing with his dry heap of scrambled eggs, Winston knew he needed help. And while he chided himself for thinking about money, Winston also realized that if the film he now held was what he thought, it could be a veritable goldmine. Altruistically, he reasoned, it might even help solve one of crime's greatest lasting mysteries. But as the nagging got worse, he realized the source of his concern. Was the film even legally his? Could he be in trouble for holding what might be considered stolen property, or images of a crime? *And what would happen when word leaked out he had it?*

Bolstering himself with one last gulp of coffee, Winston would know what to do when he got to the office. He always thought best at work. Entering his modest suburban Dallas real estate office just before 9:00 AM, Winston said "Good morning" to a few co-workers gathered around the coffee maker. He headed to his corner office, closed the door, sat down and immediately dug into his card file of contacts. "Worth...Worth....here it is." Dennis Worth, JD. Winston punched the numbers on his phone, crossed his legs and looked out the window. A female voice picked up after one ring.

"Good morning...law office of Dennis Worth. May I help you?"

"Hi, this is Ron Winston. I'm a client of Mr. Worth. Is he available?"

"I'm sorry…he's with someone right now. May I have him call you?"

Winston left his number and waited. Twenty minutes later, Dennis Worth was on the line. Winston was a conscientious real estate agent and proud he'd never been sued. But whenever the rare threat of legal action reared its ugly head, he slept better knowing he could always call the one attorney he trusted, Dennis Worth. And while there wasn't a lawsuit…at least yet…Winston disliked legalese and figured a trusted attorney was a good place to start.

"Hi Ron…what's up? I haven't heard from you in a while."

"Like you always tell me, I try to keep my nose clean. Say, I was wondering if I could talk with you in person sometime today?"

"Sounds important…or do you just have a 'hot property' you'd like to sell me?"

"It's important."

"Okay, let's see…I have a deposition at noon. How about three?"

"Terrific. I'll stop by and see you then."

A few minutes before 3:00 PM, Winston wheeled his dark blue Saab into the visitor's lot next to a particularly tall Dallas skyscraper. Passing through the building's glass doors, he wondered how his attorney would respond. Minutes later, he was escorted into Dennis Worth's office. His secretary smiled while discretely closing the door behind her. Dennis motioned Winston to a padded chair in front of his desk. The men shook hands.

"Good to see you, Ron."

"I appreciate your meeting with me so quickly."

"You chose a good time."

"Dennis, I have a question."

"That's why I'm here."

"I have what I believe could be a film of the JFK assassination."

"The Meinhofer film, right?"

"I think you mean the Zapruder film."

"Right. Excuse me. I'm not originally from here, nor am I very familiar with that case. But I know it's been examined to no end. What you have is probably a bad copy."

"No, Dennis. What I have isn't the Zapruder film, nor has it been seen by the police or the media." It was the first time Winston had ever seen his attorney speechless. After a few moments, Worth responded softly, but with a steely gaze.

"How do you know?"

"I'd never seen anything like it before last night."

"Where is it?"

"In a safe place."

Hunching forward at his oak desk, Worth rubbed a palm over the back of his other hand. "Tell me about it."

"Okay," Winston sighed, relieved at the chance to share his burden.

Worth reached into his desk and pulled out a yellow legal pad. "Alright, shoot. I mean, go ahead."

"You want the long story or the short version?"

"Everything."

Winston explained the film's discovery during a routine home inspection and proceeded to describe viewing it the previous night. As Winston spoke, his attorney scribbled on a yellow legal pad. Several times Worth looked up and slowly repeated what seemed to be near-identical questions. Winston wasn't sure what that meant, but began to wonder why this respected legal mind hadn't yet asked to view the film himself.

"Let me research how the early assassination evidence was handled and your legal standing for ownership of this film. We'll meet here at the same time tomorrow afternoon."

"So, what do you think, Dennis? Do you want to see it?"

"Ron, I want to be clear. If I take possession of your evidence, or am somehow involved in what's later construed as helping to hide it, I could be charged with obstruction of justice. So to keep the lines as bold as possible, I'm not going to view your film right now. That discussion is for later. And while I'd prefer to address your situation strictly as a hypothetical one, for the moment let's presume your film is what we think it could be. From what you've said, the film you found *might* show the John F. Kennedy assassination from a camera angle different than what has been seen.

Worth shifted in his chair. "The significance of that one fact alone could help provide new insights to a colossal mystery. However, at this point, it's too early to tell."

Worth pushed away from his desk. Leaning back, he exhaled and looked out the window. "Who developed your movie film, Ron?"

"A place here in town called Cowboy Camera."

"I'd like to apply for a 'gag order' to keep them from discussing or disclosing any film contents. But one downside of doing that is the attention it's likely to create. There's no perfect answer for certain leaks. So for now, I guess the less said, the better."

"Okay, Dennis."

"One more thing, Ron. At some point we need to discuss the matter of representation."

"I'm not lawyer-shopping here, Dennis. Are you comfortable handling this?"

Worth threw his palms out, facing Winston. "Absolutely. I'd be thrilled to do it, but there are a few remaining issues."

"What do you mean?"

"One, we need to stay in communication in real time on this. I have to be able to reach you. That means answering your phone, even if you're with clients."

"Sure. What else?"

"I'll do my best to keep costs down, but I'll need to consult experts in the field of forensic imaging and may also need to bring in an associate, both for handling research and possibly PR."

"That's fine, Dennis. Whatever you suggest."

"The plus side is that costs don't have to be prohibitive. We have access right here to an abundance of experts on the assassination and perhaps resources from the museum at Dealey Plaza. That means travel expenses should be low."

Dennis stopped speaking and sighed. "Now Ron, you're *sure* the film's in a safe place."

"Pretty sure."

"Seriously. It's evidence. As an officer of the court, I have to know if it isn't."

Ron Winston shrugged. "Okay. I promise."

"I'll take your word on it for the moment. And Ron..."

"Yeah?"

"Promise me you won't talk to *anyone* about this for now."

"I'll do my best, Dennis. Besides, my fiance' is a worry wart anyway. The less she knows about this, at least for now, the better."

"Good. This is apt to be high profile, Ron. At the end of all this, you could be a very wealthy man."

"And you could become famous."

"If this goes well, we both may be. See you tomorrow morning around 9:00, okay?"

Ron Winston looked at his watch. "I'll be here."

The two men rose, shook hands and Winston walked out of the attorney's office smiling. Violating his "No booze before 5:00 PM" rule, he stopped at the Red Steer tavern on the way home for a cold beer to celebrate what was now off his chest. Winston left the bar half an hour later and headed home, then stopped by his fiancé's house a few hours later. She greeted him at her door with a big hug. "I'll get my purse, sweetheart." A few minutes later, the two were heading into downtown Dallas.

"What kind of food sounds good to you, Suze?"

"We haven't had Chinese in a long time. Could we go to that place we ate at last time?"

"Great idea."

Half an hour later while waiting for dinner, Winston sipped his green tea and grimaced.

"What's wrong, Ron?"

"Oh, I just remembered promising my legal guy I'd avoid talking about what I told you last night. But, since you already know about it, it would be nice to talk."

"It's up to you. But I always feel better sharing, too. Did your attorney help any?"

"Yeah, he did. He has to do some research but I'm guessing it shouldn't take too long."

Winston awoke later that night in a cold sweat, the victim of a horrendous nightmare too real to ignore. In the dream, he was the only person with answers to the assassination of President John Kennedy. Driving hastily on the way to deliver details to officials, Winston missed a sharp mountain curve and drove off a cliff. Engulfed in flames, both he and details of the assassination went up in a fiery mushroom cloud.

Now awake but still breathing hard, Winston walked downstairs to the crawlspace located in his pantry closet. Tugging the handle attached to a square piece of carpeted flooring, he peered down and breathed a sigh of relief. Below in the cool environs under his house lay the movie reel, boxed and double-encased in plastic baggies. He hopped down and scooped up his treasure.

"No one would ever look here."

<u>Chapter III</u>

Picture Imperfect

Though he scheduled a day off work, Bill Maxwell was up early. He reasoned it isn't often a father can take his son to see the President of the United States. Upon learning President Kennedy would be visiting Dallas, Maxwell immediately spoke with his boss at C&J Construction to make sure he could take Friday, November 22nd off.

As a project estimator for the company, Bill Maxwell suspected business would continue to slow for what he saw as the year-end doldrums. Combined with an approaching Thanksgiving holiday the following Thursday, Maxwell figured correctly that his request for the day off would be granted. As he stood in the kitchen on November 22, 1963, his wife Sara prepared breakfast.

"Bill, he's not too young. Besides, it's *his* birthday gift."

"Sara, Teddy's eight years old. He *is* too young. I remember the goofy pictures I took with my first camera. Besides, this is a *movie* camera. I don't know why your parents even got it for him. It makes no sense for Teddy to under-expose, over-expose and double-expose film of dirt and rocks. It's an expensive toy. Wait a few years."

Bill Maxwell left the disagreement to check on their son by hollering up the staircase.

"Are you up yet, Teddy?"

"I'm awake, Dad."

"Alright, c'mon down for breakfast."

Pulling on his sweater, Teddy Maxwell's mind raced: *I've never seen a president up close before. Maybe if I'm really lucky, I could shake his hand.*

The breakfast atmosphere was electric at the Maxwell household as the family talked excitedly over scrambled eggs, bacon, oatmeal, orange juice and toast.

"I hope you two won't be late with traffic, Bill."

"Don't worry, Honey. I've carefully planned the entire trip. I am an estimator, after all. Rush hour will be over by the time we finish the half-hour drive to downtown. I figure if we leave this morning by 10:30, we'll have more than enough time to park and find a good spot. The President is supposed to drive through Dallas a little after noon."

"Hey Dad, I think I'll take my new movie camera." There was a pause at the breakfast table. Sara Maxwell looked at her husband.

"I don't know if you know how to load it yet," Bill Maxwell responded.

Teddy was quiet for a moment. "I can learn."

Bill Maxwell looked at his young son, then over to his wife and shrugged. "It's your present, Teddy. But just remember. Movie cameras don't always work well

41

right out of the box. Sometimes you have to break them in. But it might be a good time to practice."

"Okay, Dad." As Teddy excused himself from the breakfast table, Sara Maxwell looked over to her husband.

"That was awfully nice of you. What gave you a change of heart?"

Bill smiled. "I just realized that being eight years old, he'll never remember to put film in it. So why play the heavy if I don't have to? Besides, there'll be plenty of time for that when he's a teenager."

At that moment, Teddy Maxwell carefully pulled his new movie camera from beneath his bed. Later while his father shaved, Teddy inserted the roll of film his grandparents included with the gift, still buried in wrapping inside the box. Looking at the instructional diagram, he carefully threaded the film onto the pickup reel and looped it through. Teddy snapped the film cover shut, just like the picture showed. He turned the hand crank several times, then pressed the exposure button. The camera emitted a *'whirrrrr'* sound. It was now loaded and ready to film. He wrapped the leather strap around his pint-sized neck. Half an hour later with their lunches packed, Bill and young Teddy kissed Sara Maxwell goodbye and drove off together to the big city. Their drive was short, but traffic was heavier than usual.

"See all these cars, Teddy? Just like us, they're here to see President Kennedy and Governor Connally."

42

"There's a parking spot, Dad."

"I see it, Teddy."

Slamming his car door shut, Bill Maxwell walked around the vehicle and took his young son's hand. "Remember what I told you about crowds. We're likely to be in a big one today, Teddy. You need to always know where I am."

"Got it, Dad."

"Teddy, Dealey Plaza is named for George Dealey, the publisher of a local newspaper."

"Publisher? You mean he makes newspapers?"

"That's right, son."

Bill and Teddy walked through the Plaza, making their way along Houston Street.

"Where should we stand, Dad?"

"Good question, Teddy. How about the other side of the road? It's less crowded. We'll see more from there."

The two walked across the street and looked around from the north side of Main Street.

"The President will probably be passing by here, Teddy."

After a long wait, someone yelled "Here comes the President."

Gripping his movie camera tightly, Teddy pulled off the lens cover and first pointed it at his Dad, then rotated it to the correct position before aiming at the long car with flags fluttering. Bill Maxwell was busy concentrating on the parade route.

"Dang, it looks like they might turn," Bill Maxwell thought aloud. Rather than head straight on Main as he'd hoped, the presidential motorcade seemed ready to turn right onto Houston Street.

"Teddy, grab my hand…let's go toward Elm Street. The cars will probably pass by there. Then we can get a close up view."

"Okay, Dad."

As father and son headed toward Elm Street and the Stemmons freeway, the President's motorcade turned hard left onto Elm to approach them. Slowing to a walk, father and son were now within rock-throwing distance of the motorcade. Teddy resumed pointing his new camera toward the big blue limousine. Arms waved from the boat-like vehicle as it closed the distance between them. It was difficult to tell, but Teddy was sure he saw the President smile at him.

Moments later, the sound of a sudden "crack" echoed around the plaza. Oblivious to what was happening and not entirely sure where his camera pointed, young Teddy looked around but kept his finger pressed on the camera button.

As Bill Maxwell heard the first loud report, he felt what could have been a mosquito-sting on his left cheek.

Looking around, he said nothing. From that point on, everything was a surreal blur. Then came a second round of gunfire. Teddy peered through his viewfinder. After the third and fourth shots, Bill Maxwell took action.

"Get down, Teddy. Those aren't car backfires."

Looking around the plaza, Bill Maxwell intoned "Something's wrong" and gripped his son close. As they fell together on the grass, the exiting limousine's engine accelerated. A man jumped onto the car's rear fender. It was then Bill Maxwell realized someone had been shooting at the president. His president. He rose and brushed grass off his son. Shortly after the limousine sped off, a police officer ran up to Teddy and covered the camera's lens with one hand.

"Did you get anything on film? If you did, it's evidence."

Bill Maxwell pulled the patrolman to one side and whispered so his son couldn't hear him.

"He's eight years old, officer. There's no film in his camera—he doesn't even know how to load it yet. Open it if you want, but then the kid will know his old man's too cheap to pay for film."

As a siren went off in the distance, the officer looked over Bill's shoulder. There stood Teddy, kicking the grass. Now running in the direction of the siren's wail, the officer shouted over his shoulder: "On my salary, I understand."

Bill Maxwell walked over to his son.

"Am I in trouble, Dad?"

"No, Teddy. Not at all."

Teddy looked up at his father, now weeping uncontrollably. It was a moment neither would forget. All around were speechless bystanders, mouths agape. Moments later, Bill Maxwell took his son's hand and held him close.

"I'm sorry, Teddy. The world can be a scary place. Let's go home and see Mommy. It's been a long day."

The ride home became longer once Bill Maxwell turned on the car radio. The first voice they heard was terse.

"This is a radio news bulletin. It is being reported that President Kennedy has been shot in Dealey Plaza. We have no word on his condition. Please stay tuned and we will provide updates as they are available. We now return you to our regular programming."

Once home, Teddy, his father and mother huddled before their small black and white living room television. Several hours later, President Kennedy was pronounced dead. The grief-filled days that followed were not confined to the Maxwell household. As his body lie in state at the U.S. Capitol building, an entire nation mourned both the loss of President Kennedy and the near-murder of Texas Governor John Connally. It had all happened on a beautiful November day in Dallas.

For the third night in a row after the assassination, little Teddy Maxwell had a hard time sleeping. In the middle of the night, all he could think about was his father's reaction to the events in Dallas. What they'd experienced was catastrophic, yet in his eight year old mind, Bill Maxwell's response loomed equally large. "If Dad is worried, it must be really bad," was all Teddy reasoned.

Previously a constant source of fun, jokes and optimism, Bill Maxwell became moody and withdrawn. During one father-son disagreement, young Teddy watched his Dad erupt into tears for no apparent reason and leave the room. Teddy hoped to make it better and wanted his old Dad back, so he devised a plan. Teddy would throw away any trace of what they'd witnessed. That would fix everything, he reasoned.

On a morning after his father left for work and his mother was gardening, Teddy carefully reached under his bed and opened his still-new camera box. Leading with his chin in deliberation, the young boy clutched the box to his chest and scurried out of the room into the hall. He dragged a chair directly below the attic access just like he saw his dad do several days earlier to retrieve stored Christmas ornaments.

"Except this box will never be opened again," he insisted. Jumping up onto the chair, Teddy pushed open the square wood cover with a broom handle. He proceeded to throw the camera box—as hard as his little league arm could—through the opening, before dropping the broom handle to the ground.

###

It was a grey and unseasonably cool Texas morning when real estate agent Ron Winston arrived at the law office of Dennis Worth.

"Ron, meet H. Randall Mackey. Randall is a forensic photographic specialist. He has experience working on weighty criminal cases and is considered an expert witness. As we discussed, he's someone I've asked to consult with us on your film."

"Pleased to meet you, Ron."

"Likewise."

Randall Mackey was a tidy, wiry man, due in part to his penchant for marathons. He wore khaki pants, a blue button down oxford with bow tie and carried a large water bottle. Mackey cleared his throat nervously and began speaking in a quiet tone.

"From what Dennis has told me, Ron, the film you have may provide a different angle of the Kennedy assassination than commonly recognized."

Ron Winston smiled in agreement, as Mackey looked expectedly at both men before continuing. "Did you bring it with you?"

Worth interjected on behalf of his client: "Randall, given the extraordinary significance of what we may be dealing with here, we hoped to first speak with you hypothetically and off-the-record. I presume you're okay with signing a confidentiality agreement?"

"Absolutely. I'm honored and humbled for any chance to work with you both on a project like this. It really is a once-in-a-lifetime opportunity. It's also important that you both feel confident with my handling of the film, since the JFK assassination is a case-study on how poorly forensic evidence can be handled and preserved. Plus, the chain of custody is crucial."

Worth nodded as Mackey continued. "Since I haven't seen it yet, perhaps this is a good time for me to background you both on issues surrounding the JFK assassination and what I expect to be looking for in your film. It's a fascinating, but arduous history, so I'll give you the abbreviated version. Before we even examine the footage you have, it's crucial for you to understand the assassination's elements to grasp the significance of potential new evidence."

Winston and Worth smiled at each other.

"In a nutshell, gentlemen, this could be huge. I've researched not only how the Kennedy assassination films were handled, but also other less-known films chronicling the event."

Worth grimaced before speaking. "There's more than one film?"

Mackey smiled. "You're not alone; most people aren't aware. At least five better-known films of the JFK assassination are known to exist… at least, apparently until now."

Ron Winston's face scrunched up in an unknowing, prune-like grimace. "What effect does that have on anything new that's discovered?"

Mackey's hands turned upward as he shrugged. "Depends. But there's no doubt anything new could be worth a lot...in terms of potential forensic evidence, historical value and sheer publicity. But first, we need to analyze it and follow where things lead. Like most criminal evidence, it's similar to working on a jigsaw puzzle. The main difference here is that it's high profile, so we need to do everything right. We're working with a pastiche' of evidence, if you will. If it fits, we use it. If it doesn't, we move on."

"Whatever you recommend, Randall," Worth interjected. "You're the expert here. But I have one other question at the moment."

"Sure. What is it, Dennis?"

"I don't want to jump the gun, but how much could this film be worth?"

"Again, it depends. Aside from content, what makes any of these films so important is exclusivity. Each film provides details others don't, some more than others."

"Feel free to elaborate on that," Worth suggested.

Mackey pushed his eyeglasses high on his nose. "The JFK assassination occurred mere yards from amateur photographer and businessman Abraham Zapruder. The term 'Zapruder film' is a moniker coined for his key piece of evidence of that infamous afternoon. Thus, Zapruder's name remains forever linked to the president's murder in Dallas. For nearly half a century, the Zapruder film has been considered the 'Rosetta Stone' of the Kennedy assassination. It shows much of the Kennedy assassination, frame by frame and in considerable detail. Of the available films to date, it's by far the best known and the 'gold standard' of forensic evidence on the assassination for several good reasons. That's because it gives a relatively complete account of the event and was taken at close range."

Randall Mackey stood up and looked out the window before resuming. "Angles of shots fired will be forever debated due to the Zapruder film. Yet it's also considered a clear enough record of the event to calculate things like the timing between shot intervals since we know the movie camera's speed."

Mackey took a deep breath and continued. "As you know, the JFK assassination has turned into a cottage industry. You've seen the talk shows. Everyone from serious forensic scientists and medical-legal analysts, to all kinds of crackpots keep offering theories on the shooting. It's easy to see why, because the Kennedy assassination is the ultimate 'whodunit.' Who killed the world's most powerful man? Add the fact that during critical moments of Zapruder's film, a street sign obstructs the camera's view. And because the gunner or gunners are out of sight of Zapruder's camera, it becomes a real mystery to know precisely what happened. That's also why other issues, like the number of shots fired, is still debated."

Transfixed, Winston marveled at Mackey's confidence, grasp of history and the possibility that together they all be part of answering some long-awaited questions. Mackey looked at Winston and Worth.

"Are you guys still with me?"

"Yup," Worth replied. Winston weighed in with "Absolutely."

"Okay, but just stop me if you have questions. Anyway as I was saying, as good as it is, even the Zapruder film doesn't show everything. And that's crucial…because the especially vexing part is what it *doesn't* show….namely, things like what's happening *behind* Zapruder as the shots are fired. For decades, many have speculated about a purported shooter on the 'Grassy Knoll,' which is behind Zapruder as he filmed the assassination."

"I saw the movie *JFK*," Winston volunteered.

"Then you have an idea, albeit the Hollywood version, of what I'm talking about," Mackey replied. "So as Mr. Zapruder filmed the shooting with his soundless movie camera, some eye and ear-witnesses noted shots fired from behind the 'Grassy Knoll.' Various photos show bystanders across Dealey Plaza running and pointing in that direction. This is corroborated by both the Warren Commission Report and acoustic tests from the congressional re-opening of the case. Both suggest the possibility of a second gunman. But there are also some problems, because some who witnessed the very same event pointed in different directions, possibly because of acoustics in Dealey Plaza, or perhaps due to multiple gunmen."

Mackey took a long drink of water and resumed. "It's also important to realize that both the government's Warren Commission Report and a much later congressional investigation of the shooting suggest what was called a 'conspiracy.' Mr. Zapruder himself told officials he heard shots fired from behind him, which would have been the grassy knoll, not above and in front of Zapruder—which is from the direction of the Texas Schoolbook Depository."

"But other evidence provides tantalizing clues, too…especially an obscure home movie known as the 'Orville Nix' film. In Nix's film we see Mrs. Kennedy climb on back of the president's vehicle after the shooting. It's also the only movie with a decent view of the 'Grassy Knoll.' Enhancements show what some interpret as a muzzle blast from that direction. There's another movie of the Kennedy assassination called the 'Mary Muchmore' film, with some helpful information."

Mackey placed his index fingers together steeple-like, and lowered his voice. "There's much at stake here, gentlemen. Bottom line, no single record of the event definitively confirms the issues debated for decades. Like was there a shooter on the grassy knoll? Or a second gunman in the Texas Schoolbook Depository? A possible cover-up? With modern film enhancement techniques, your film *could* be the one to determine these questions. So let's walk through what we already know."

Mackey switched on his laptop to reveal a computer slideshow presentation. An aerial photo of

Dealey Plaza appeared on a wall screen. Mackey's laser pointer highlighted an area on the image as he resumed speaking. "Zapruder filmed the presidential motorcade snaking through Dealey Plaza from here, using his Bell & Howell movie camera."

Randall Mackey looked over at Worth, now taking notes furiously on a yellow legal pad. "I realize there's quite a bit of information here guys, so tell me if you want me to slow down, or need a break."

Worth stopped writing and looked up. "Keep going, Randall—we can take it. Besides, this is a lot more interesting than my old law school classes on contracts." Winston smiled, glad he was a real estate agent and not a lawyer.

Randall Mackey cleared his throat and smiled. "Okay. As crucial footage of the JFK murder, Zapruder's amateur film provides reliable forensic evidence, such as the shooter or shooter's timing, all calculable in frames per second. Monumental assumptions about the meticulously scrutinized shooting are based upon what happened during each frame of Zapruder's film. But for each question seemingly answered from painstaking examination and analysis of this key piece of evidence, several more are raised."

Mackey coughed and took another drink of water before continuing. "Bottom line, there's much the Zapruder film doesn't provide. Some astonishingly basic issues remain elusive. For example, was the President shot from behind or the front? How many shots were fired? How many gunmen? Conflict and debate on these issues continue to make this among the most compelling and baffling mysteries of all time. Issues not decisively settled through examination of the film nag critics and proponents alike."

"Why haven't so many questions on this assassination been adequately answered, Randall?" Winston asked.

"An official government investigation on the shooting promised to resolve them. As I've mentioned, an in-depth study of the Kennedy assassination became known as the 'Warren Report.' It was a blue ribbon panel under the auspices of the Warren Commission, headed by then chief Supreme Court justice Earl Warren."

"Warren moved the court to the left," Worth opined.

"That's correct," Mackey said. "But political leanings aside, the Warren Commission was no body of partisan lightweights. Joining Supreme Court chief justice Warren were U.S. Congressman and future U.S. President Gerald Ford, plus legal counsel and future U.S. Senator Arlen Spector. Another commission member was Allen Dulles, the former CIA director fired by John F. Kennedy after the botched October, 1962 'Bay of Pigs' invasion of Cuba. That operation was attempted by fiercely nationalistic anti-Castro ex-pats, organized and financed by the CIA."

"Sounds heavy," Winston interjected.

"Oh yeah, but there's more," Mackey said. "The Warren Commission was also criticized for indeterminate findings and then sealing certain information for decades into the future. Imagine burying evidence on this. Because of such curious behavior, there's little wonder that even now, polls consistently report most Americans believe a conspiracy took place in Dallas on November 22, 1963. There's also a cultural context to the JFK assassination. Kennedy's death is often cited as America's 'loss of innocence.' Ask any older adult where they were on November 22, 1963 and chances are, they remember."

Mackey looked at Winston and Worth before continuing.

"Now here's where it gets dicey, guys. Key issues in the report remain hotly debated. As a result, they reinforce the public perception of a conspiracy and cover-up. One troubling hypothesis includes the infamous 'single bullet' theory. It suggests only one shot caused the carnage on that fateful day. Details about the infamous 'Grassy Knoll,' where numerous witnesses to the assassination claimed a shot was fired, were never conclusive. And mystery still shrouds the 'pristine bullet' retrieved from the dead President's gurney. That one's a problem because few expect a bullet going through so many people to remain undamaged and weigh more later than before it was fired."

Worth and Winston shook their heads, incredulous.

"Further complicating the situation, gentlemen, was the reversal of several Zapruder film frames while in FBI hands, along with purposely-destroyed autopsy records by the very physician conducting the procedure.

That physician even changed the location of the bullet wound, allegedly due to pressure from 'shadowy men' standing by during the autopsy. But perhaps most puzzling of all was the order given to the president's secret service detail to 'stand down.' This forced them to refrain from certain protective activities designed to keep the president safe in Dallas."

Mackey strolled over to the table near the front of the room.

"It really is hard to know how best to sift through so much potentially relevant material. Alleged shooter Lee Harvey Oswald said he was only a 'patsy' for the crime and not the one responsible for the president's death. Oswald himself was killed soon afterward by Jack Ruby, a nightclub owner with known mob ties. Stranger still, Ruby actually knew Oswald and after killing Oswald, Ruby died in prison. He took his true motive for shooting the president's accused killer with him to the grave.

But there's more. Controversy still swirls on whether a mail-order rifle fired allegedly fired by assassin Lee Harvey Oswald could have been sufficiently accurate...or the action fast enough...to hit a moving target under the circumstances. All sides have their pet theories. Yet one central question looms largest of all and the answer is key to solve countless details: Who gained with the president's death? More than one powerful organization wanted President Kennedy killed. Each had motive. Each had means. And each could have found Dallas the perfect opportunity. So is it any wonder that, decades later, we continue to probe among these usual suspects?"

As Mackey continued, he hooked his right index finger across fingers of his left hand in succession, enumerating potentially guilty parties. "And here they are."

"One, the Mafia. Two, Cuban leader Fidel Castro. Three, the Soviet Union. Four, Southerners angry with the Kennedy administration's interference in 'state's rights' issues like racial integration. Five, rogue elements of the CIA, thought to support the U.S. 'military-industrial complex,' allegedly for fear of a quick pullout from Vietnam. Or sixth, was it simply FBI ineptness?"

"Any others?" Worth queried.

"Yes, there are others, Mackey continued. But most are considered marginal at best, long shots at worst."

"Try us," Winston responded.

"Well guys, one theory has future president Lyndon Johnson as the beneficiary of Kennedy's death and therefore somehow complicit. Johnson was a Texan and in a unique position to influence important factors during the president's visit on Johnson's Texas turf. Plus, LBJ and JFK weren't exactly best friends. But my spin on perhaps the most interesting possibility aside from the usual suspects is Greek shipping tycoon Aristotle Onassis."

Worth raised his eyebrows. "Onassis? That is interesting."

"Right," Mackey replied. "The reasoning goes that because he ended up marrying Jackie Kennedy, albeit years after JFK was killed, Onassis was a direct, though belated beneficiary of JFK's death. Plus, as a billionaire, he certainly had the resources to do it."

Mackey tapped the table in front of him. "But aside from these long-shots—if you'll pardon the tasteless pun—to many, the Mob is a perennial odds-on favorite of suspected participants in the JFK assassination sweepstakes...and for good reason. That's because as an energetic United States Attorney General inside his brother's cabinet, Robert Kennedy zealously prosecuted high profile Mafia figures. Plus, Mob surveillance tapes even reveal discussions of President Kennedy's murder. Adding fuel to that fire is the President's alleged dalliance with Mafia kingpin Sam Giancana's girlfriend, Judith Campbell Exner, who is said to have passed messages between the president and mobster Giancana."

Mackey cleared his throat. "But Castro is also a strong contender for involvement in the JFK assassination. President Kennedy's botched attempt to overthrow Cuba's then-youthful communist leader during the 'Bay of Pigs' invasion made Kennedy a logical target for Fidel Castro's 'hit squads.'"

"As the crucial hour for the invasion approached, Kennedy had second thoughts and reduced the force used to invade Cuba. The coup attempt failed. So instead of de-fanging the communist leader on America's doorstep who was supported by Moscow with materiel, food and missiles, a now-energized Castro had plenty of reason to even the score."

Mackey looked at Winston and Worth, then shrugged. "Given the Cold War rhetoric and Soviet Premier Nikita Kruschev's promise to the United States that 'We will bury you,' Mother Russia is another candidate suspected to have the motive, means and opportunity to kill the President. But there is no 'smoking gun' that points for certain to Moscow. Upon examining alleged assassin Lee Harvey Oswald's ties to the US military, Cuba and the Soviet Union, the murderer's trail gets murky, indeed."

"After leaving the US Marine Corps, Oswald defects to the Soviet Union, then takes a Russian bride. Before long, he grows disenchanted with the gap between communism's idealism and the impoverished reality he witnesses firsthand. So Oswald returns to the United States and proceeds to protest on behalf of an organization called the 'Free Play for Cuba' committee.

"Another Cuban connection, but with a Russian twist," Winston commented.

"Exactly," Mackey agreed, before resuming. "Complicating matters further are bureaucratic turf wars between the Kennedy administration and FBI chief J. Edgar Hoover, who harbored animosity toward the Kennedy brothers. Hoover fought hard to maintain control of the bureau he built and didn't appreciate Bobby Kennedy's 'nosing around.'"

Worth raised his hand. "So where does this all leave us, Randall?"

"I've outlined the alliance between La Cosa Nostra, also known as the 'Mafia,' the 'Mob' or 'The Commission,' and Cuba. At one time, the Mafia had a tight grip on Cuba. But to answer your question, it's really quite basic. I believe one theory has been overlooked. That theory suggests the Mob and Castro simply joined forces. And given Castro's connection with his fellow communist allies like the Soviet Union, it connects the dots to some of the most likely suspects."

"Doesn't that seem kind of far-fetched, Randall?" Worth asked.

Mackey grew animated. "Look. There may not be a 'smoking gun,' but the close link between Castro and the USSR is provable. The Soviets are suspected of sending Castro's government the equivalent of one million dollars a week in subsidies for *years*. Cuba was a proxy government that did the Soviets' bidding. So in essence, whatever Moscow wanted, Castro co-operated with…potentially including the death of our president."

Worth shrugged at Mackey. "So, what's the next step?"

"To evaluate each likely hypothesis, I need the film. From there, it could take anywhere from a week to a month to copy, restore and examine. From there, we'll know what we're dealing with."

Glancing at his client, Worth said "Ron, you okay with that?"

Winston studied Worth and Mackey before speaking. "Sure. I'll have it here. Just say the word."

"I'll pick it up myself, Ron," volunteered Mackey. "Just call me."

###

Having lost big earlier in the week at a Vegas poker table, Wayne Schaefer was still moping, days later. Barricaded in his den, he arose from his worn leather chair and picked up the phone on the third ring. In no mood for small talk, his raspy bark simply announced "Schaefer." The young voice on the other end of the phone spoke rapidly.

"Mr. Schaefer? This is Skip Hollister."

Schaefer's gruff demeanor turned sunny as he fought the urge to say "I told you so." "Skip. Hey...I *knew* you'd call. It's been what, a few weeks since we talked? What turned you around?"

"Actually, Mr. Schaefer, I haven't changed my mind...but I would like to meet with you. It's important."

"Something wrong?"

"I could sure use your advice. Can we meet?"

"Uh, sure, Skip. When?"

"Would now work?"

"Sounds important."

"It is."

Schaefer's thoughts remained charitable toward the hapless young man in a dead-end job. He'd once been in the same position himself and took pity on the kid. But so urgent was Skip's tone, Schaefer decided to meet somewhere other than his own home, at least until he determined the precise nature of the problem. Still hungry after a light dinner, Schaefer's stomach now churned at the thought of his favorite French restaurant. Schaefer had been looking for an excuse to get out of the house anyway and disliked eating alone. Plus, his favorite restaurant's view of the city made meals there an event.

"Okay, Skip. How about 'Baccarat?' This late in the evening, we can probably get a table."

"Sure thing. Tell me where it is and I'll meet you there."

"You can't miss it. It's right off the Stemmons Freeway near the golf course. Look for the bright red neon sign."

"Oh, I know where that is. I really appreciate this, Mr. Schaefer."

"Sure, kid. See you in half an hour."

Backing his black Suburban out of the driveway, a dozen jumbled thoughts entered Wayne Schaefer's mind. He figured the kid's problem boiled down to trouble with girls, money or the law. "I hope it's not drugs," Schaefer pondered. Given sparse after-hours traffic and oldies jazz on the radio, he made the drive in an enjoyable 25 minutes. Waiting in the restaurant's wood paneled foyer with computer notebook in tow was none other than Skip Hollister. It was nice to see his son's boyhood friend smiling for a change.

"Skip. Glad to see you again."

The two men shook hands as Skip responded softly.

"Thanks for meeting with me right away, Mr. Schaefer. I haven't been able to sleep."

"No problem. Glad to help out. Let's get a table."

The mustached Maitre'd arrived as if on cue, his accent thick as filet mignon. "Bonjour, gentlemen. How may I help you this evening?"

"A window booth for two, please."

The Maitre'd arched his bushy eyebrows, his animated voice concerned. "You have reservations, no?"

"Not exactly, but I figured there'd be no problem this late."

The Maitre'd's once-hopeful look deflated instantaneously. "I'm afraid we're full until 10 PM, M'sieur. There ees a convention. Perhaps zee bar?"

"Sorry to hear that," Schaefer replied. Reaching into his coat pocket, he deftly placed a fifty dollar bill in the man's palm. Bowing deeply to his new found friend, the Maitre'd replied: "I promise to see what I can do, M'sieur."

The Maitre'd was back in 10 seconds. "M'sieur, due to a most fortuitous cancellation, I was able to find *just* the booth for you. This way, please."

"Thanks, Pierre."

"De rien, je vous en prie, M'sieur," replied the host with his most gracious 'You're welcome.' Passing through a packed dinner crowd, the two men were escorted to a private booth overlooking the lights of Dallas. Once the Beaujolais was poured and their main courses were ordered, Schaefer could no longer contain his curiosity.

"So, Skip. Thinking about a career move? And why are you so eager to talk to me about it?"

Looking down, Skip Hollister gripped the base of his wine glass with one hand and ran a finger up the stem.

"Mr. Schaefer, I'm going to play it straight. Since I didn't follow my Dad's career path, he and I don't exactly see eye-to-eye anymore. So while I appreciate your offer of help, I don't expect you to agree with everything I'm about to say. All I ask is for your ear and advice."

Schaefer looked at his protégé and leaned forward, his forehead now directly over a tiny plate of hors d'oeuvres between them.

"Sure kid," he replied. "But you have to understand one thing." Schaefer tapped his massive forefinger on the starched white tablecloth for emphasis. "Given my line of work, there's very little that surprises me. So to be frank, you're probably overreacting."

Hollister said nothing. Stabbing a canape' with his fork, Schaefer popped it into his waiting mouth and chewed slowly, smiling as he looked directly at the young man across the table.

"So what's this all about, Skip? Now you've got me curious. Let's hear it."

Hollister cleared his throat, looked around the dining room and lowered his voice.

"Okay...so I'm at work a few weeks ago. A guy I've never seen comes in and drops off an 8mm roll of movie film for developing. No problem, right? So, I spot-check it for exposure, since amateurs rarely know how to use a light meter. That's even if they have one, right? Anyway, I see some really weird stuff on it."

Schaefer stopped buttering his baguette and looked up. "Weird? What do you mean, weird?"

"I've spot-checked miles of film and this was *not* normal. Anyway, as I run through this roll, I realize a lot of amateur filmmakers are getting inventive these days. So now I'm thinking 'Hey, maybe this is an artsy horror film.' You know, like the 'Blair Witch Project.'"

Schaefer raised his hand.

"Skip, wait. I'm your Dad's age. I hope you understand that other than like 'Frankenstein' or

'Dracula,' I've never watched a horror film. So what's this all about?"

Hollister's pasty face turned even paler as his voice shook. "A guy in a car is shot."

In the restaurant's dim light, Schaefer briefly shifted his eyes to his rapidly depleting glass of wine and exhaled deeply.

"Anything else?"

Skip shifted in his seat. "Yes…just please understand I'm not making this up…but I have to tell somebody. I can't get the images out of my head."

Schaefer nodded once and slowly looked up at his son's friend, palms open. "Okay Skip, try me."

Skip Hollister stared at his own hands spread on the table while he spoke. "With the dark limousine and flags on the hood, I could swear it looked like footage I've seen of President Kennedy here in Dallas…but from a totally different camera angle."

The normally unflappable Wayne Schaefer opened his mouth, yet no sound came out. He stood up, rapidly scanned the dim restaurant over the top of their booth and sat down.

"Did anyone follow you here?"

Hollister was unnerved to see the dad of his boyhood friend change from dismissive to dead serious in a single heartbeat.

"No. But I wasn't looking, either. Like I said, I don't know what to make of this all."

Schaefer cleared his throat before speaking.

"Okay, Skip. You have my attention. When it comes to this kind of thing, I can be very serious, too. So where's the film now and who's this guy who brought it in," Schaefer demanded in a forceful, hushed tone.

Hollister responded in a strained whisper. "Like I said, I'd never seen him before, but figured you'd want to check him out."

Pulling a wrinkled wad from his back pocket, Skip Hollister passed it face down across the table.

"So I brought this. It's a photocopy of his driver's license. We require a copy whenever anyone rents our projectors."

Schaefer grabbed the document and angled it toward the table candle. After studying it, he looked up in pained bewilderment.

"Never heard of him."

"Me either, Mr. Schaefer."

Patting the document he held with the back of his meaty right hand, Schaefer's eyes were intent. "Look, Skip; I may be furloughed for the moment, but why did you wait to tell me about this? You know you can trust me. Your Dad and I watched each others' backsides for years. We were like brothers. Besides, I *still* have connections, practically to the top."

Hollister shook his head in silence.

Schaefer flicked the paper with his index finger. "But *this* guy, *whoever* he is, I have no clue. And if this is a bogus driver's license and you last saw him a week or two ago, he could very hard to track by now."

Skip defensively shrugged his shoulders. "I had to think it over. Only after the film had been picked up did I seriously begin to think it was real...and that maybe I should tell someone."

Schaefer folded the paper carefully and placed it inside his breast jacket pocket. "So, kid. When did you decide to call me?"

Hollister grew thoughtful. "Well, it bothered me that I might be the only person in a position to do something if it *was* real. Then I realized real or not, this wasn't a secret I was willing to risk keeping...no matter how stupid I might look. I did do something else, though."

Schaefer eyed Hollister cautiously. "What's that?" he ventured. Hollister pulled a small disc out of his lightweight jacket and presented it to Schaefer. "Here's one of the two copies I made of the film. I figured you'd want to check it out."

Schaefer smiled, but couldn't believe his ears. It was all he could do to maintain his composure as Skip dropped the potentially priceless film into his palm. Gripping it tightly, he quickly placed it into his breast pocket. Skip shifted his computer on the restaurant table and turned it on.

"Mr. Schaefer, in case you were wondering what's on it, I can show you."

Schaefer looked suspiciously around the room. "Can you turn that around so others can't see it?"

"Sure," Hollister replied softly. "No worries. It has a privacy screen on it, so unless someone is sitting where you are, they won't see it."

Hollister turned the notebook computer around to face Schaefer and hit a button. Images moved on the screen before him. Moments later, Schaefer saw flags fluttering on an approaching dark limousine.

"I've never seen film from this angle," Schaefer whispered. Next appeared the image of a woman wearing a pink pillbox hat. "And there's Jackie."

Cautiously looking around the room, Schaefer turned the notebook around.

"I've seen enough for now."

"There's more," commented Hollister.

"Skip. A few things. One, I know how that film ends. And two, at this point, it really doesn't matter what I think anyway. I need to have this reviewed by our forensics people."

Schaefer grew increasingly serious.

"Alright, Skip. Here's the deal. I greatly appreciate your sharing this information with me.

However, for your own safety, I don't like the idea of this information floating around."

"You're the only person I've talked with about this, Mr. Schaefer."

"How many copies are there of this out there right now, Skip?"

"Well, there's one copy with the Winston guy who brought the film in, and now you have a copy, and of course what you just viewed on my notebook here."

Schaefer rose from their booth just as the meal arrived. "Good thinking, Skip. This could help a lot. Thanks for bringing it to me."

Pulling out his wallet, he looked over at Skip. "Sorry, I have to go. This should cover it."

Two hundreds landed neatly on the table atop an untouched baguette. By the time Schaefer reached the exit door, Hollister was devouring the first of two meals that night his nervous stomach would keep down. Once outside, Schaefer breathed in the light evening mist. He began jogging to his vehicle in the restaurant parking lot, both hands covering the film in his breast jacket pocket. Unlocking the car door, he reached underneath the driver's seat and pressed a dime-sized button as a tiny headset dropped from overhead into his waiting hand.

Turning onto East Lamar Boulevard, Schaefer snaked the device snugly in his ear and connected it to an encrypted two-way communication console under the dashboard. The entire mechanism was plugged into a satellite phone antenna, now silently rising from the car roof. It was synchronized to aim for the closest available orbiting communications satellite.

Before he could say 'Testing,' a dark blue light in front of him confirmed the encrypted satellite patch was complete to his supervising CIA case officer in the Maryland countryside. With two time zones separating them, it was now just past midnight on the east coast. Schaefer pressed firmly on the transmitter with his free hand and spoke in a slow, measured tone.

"Lancer. Lancer—do you read?" Moments later, a relaxed voice hinting a southern accent responded. "Lancer? Well, now.....It's been quite a while."

Lancer had been the US Secret Service code name for President John F. Kennedy. It stemmed, logically enough, from the then-chief executive's fascination with all things Camelot. And while that particular moniker hadn't been uttered by members of American intelligence agencies for a very long time, it remained a well-known part of "spook," or spy lore. Many operatives deep inside the U.S. government believed someday, somehow, the slate would finally be wiped clean on the unresolved assassination that tarnished their respective agencies, including the CIA and FBI, so many decades earlier.

The disembodied voice at the other end of the line was plain-spoken. "Let's start with what you've got."

"If justice is truly sweet, let's just say we now have an elephant-sized chocolate bar in our hands."

"Care to elaborate?"

"I just received newly discovered photographic evidence on what appears to be the JFK assassination," Schaefer stated with buoyant emphasis.

"Wow. This oughta get the attention of at least a fewer of the higher-ups."

"Dang right," voiced Schaefer. "Now after decades of work, worry and waiting, let's hope it's still not too late to solve this one."

Through sporadic interference, a loud crackle sounded before the voice returned. "What's your location?"

"Metropolitan Dallas."

"Coordinates received. Rendevous arranged. You're fixed for access point 7-1-1 at 0200."

Schaefer responded with a simple 'Out' and punched the vehicle's accelerator. "It's going to be a long night," Schaefer smiled.

Chapter IV

Grassy Knolls & Russian Moles

At 10:00 AM on a pleasant Texas Friday, real estate agent Ron Winston strolled arm in arm with his elderly client Emma Scofield. It was their first house-hunting tour in two decades. The eighty-seven-year-old widow had been his very first customer. Now all these years later and with her husband gone, she remained his most loyal.

"Remember when you told me to put my garden on the other side of the garage, Ron? I'm so glad I listened to you. They widened the road...it would have killed my lilacs!"

"I remember, Emma. I remember," Winston said while patting her hand.

Emma Scofield was now mostly housebound. These days, even garden work was out of the question. So when she called Winston several months earlier, he expected her to move into a retirement village. Not Emma. She envied her sister's freedom from home maintenance in a one-level condo. Before long, she was on the phone with 'Real Estate Ron' to see if a similar property might be available.

Winston appreciated her business, but Emma remained far more than a sales commission and reminded him of his long-departed grandmother. After receiving her phone call to find a condo, Winston confided to a coworker: "Emma's a rare treat. I don't usually get to work with buyers this age. Plus, she can pay in cash."

Walking back to the car, Winston respectfully opened Emma's car door and helped her into the front passenger seat. The older woman looked up at him as he buckled her seat belt.

"Just like old times, Ron."

"That's right Emma…but remember; you're not getting older, you're getting better."

Winston rarely laid it on thick, but given his fondness for Emma, he was happy to add an extra coat or two. Handing her the cane she now used, he returned to the driver's side, opened his car door and sat down. He reached for his sunglasses on the dashboard.

"That's weird," Winston mumbled as he turned to Emma. "I *always* leave them on the dashboard." Looking up into his rear view mirror, he saw a masked face but little else. Next came Emma's scream, followed by a clap of thunder against his right temple. Winston thought he'd pass out from the pain. Then came the shaking and a strange voice.

"Where is it?"

"Where's what?"

"You know what I'm here for. Don't play with me."

The attacker's grip squeezed Winston's neck as if made of soft clay. About to pass out, Winston braced for another strike and tensed his right arm. When the anticipated jolt wasn't repeated, Winston reached behind and grabbed for whatever he could. His hand was soon attached to a long arm in a death grip with a .357 magnum revolver. Pulling fiercely, the firearm quivered in front of his face.

A bright patch of red liquid gleamed on the weapon's cylinder. *No wonder it hurt so much*, Winston thought. From the handgun's angle in his attacker's gorilla-like paw, Winston caught a glimpse of the cannon-sized rounds in the chamber. Emma alternately screamed and poked the intruder about the head and shoulders with her cane. The commotion began generating attention from approaching passersby.

Firmly gripping the intruder's arm with both hands, Winston clamped down with all his might and pulled hard, pounding the resistant fist against the steering wheel. The weapon dropped in his lap before landing on the car floor under the brake pedal. Before snatching the gun, a quick backward motion saw Winston forcefully deliver a tidy knuckle sandwich into the assailant's chops. As Winston deftly slid the attacker's heavy artillery into his waistband, the bad guy dropped with a thud against the back car door. Winston looked over to his client.

"Emma, keep an eye open for any others while I check this guy out."

Mouth agape, she simply stared at her normally mild-mannered real estate agent. Winston got out of the car, opened the back door and watched his attacker fall half-way out of the vehicle in a crumpled heap. Grabbing the sprawled figure by the lapel of his tweed jacket, he shook hard.

"Who are you?"

There was no response. Winston shook some more.

"Who're you working for?"

The guy was out cold. Winston opened the attacker's jacket and fished around for a wallet...anything. He found a single page, neatly folded.

"What's this?"

Unfolding the sheet revealed a map, clearly annotated in Cyrillic lettering. Circled in red at the center of the page was Winston's home address.

"Some Russian wants me...and probably dead. But who?"

Winston pulled the out-cold assailant up by his own limp arms and slipped under him. With the thug slung over his back, Winston crab-walked Quasimodo-like to the curb. He dumped the attacker on a grassy knoll, out of sight next to a hedge. Ceremoniously dusting his hands off, Winston looked over to his bewildered client, then returned to the car.

"C'mon, Emma. We've got a house to tour."

Given Winston's newfound nonchalance, Emma began to wonder if it all might have just been a prank.

"What was that all about, Ron?"

As they headed to the next property on their tour, Winston turned to his client and smiled.

"Emma, you may not realize just how fiercely competitive real estate sales is. In this market, some agents will practically kill for a new client."

Winston was still breathing hard but didn't want to further alarm his senior guest. Arriving at their destination, he walked up to the house and opened the lockbox hung on the front doorknob. Gradually events of the day started to make sense to him. Winston silently recited every gumshoe detective's list to narrow a universe of suspects.

Means. Motive. Opportunity. Whoever it is, they've gone to a great deal of trouble for something. But what?

Sliding the house key into the lock, Winston opened the door and announced "real estate agent," to warn anyone in the house he was there on legitimate business, not breaking and entering. It was a precaution he performed routinely ever since walking in on some unsuspecting homeowners in various states of undress. Hearing and seeing nothing, he motioned Emma inside. As Winston's thoughts raced, it hit him.

Cyrillic lettering. Weapons. The FILM. Russians want the film. And the only way they'll get it is through me.

Winston murmured "I need to talk to Dennis." After his elderly client stepped into the cozy condo, Winston returned to the porch, pulled out his cell phone and proceeded to dial his attorney. "I'll be right with you, Emma."

"Hello—Law office of Dennis Worth."

"Hi, I'm a client and need to speak with Dennis."

"He's in a meeting at the moment."

"It's urgent."

"Please hold."

"Dennis speaking."

"Dennis. I was just attacked."

"Ron. Is that you?"

"Yes."

"What happened?"

"Some guy was lying in wait for me inside my own car."

"Are you okay?"

"Shaken up, but he's the one far worse off."

"Was it a random thing?"

"You mean like a carjacking?"

"Right."

"Not unless assaulting real estate agents is the latest hobby of Russian spies."

"Russian spies?"

"Call it a hunch. The guy had a map written in Cyrillic and my house was circled in red."

"Whoa."

"What do I do?"

"Where's your attacker?"

"Probably still on the grass where I left him."

"What happened to him?"

"Let's just say he'll hurt when he wakes up."

"Alright. And he attacked you first?"

"Definitely. I have a witness."

"And you were in fear for your life?"

"Absolutely."

"Okay. If we report it, be prepared for a lot of things to happen very fast. If you're not in any danger at the moment, we can talk when you have time to come in."

"Okay. Thanks, Dennis."

"Bye."

Re-entering the charming condo, Winston earnestly attempted to hide his concern. Minutes later, he was pleasantly surprised at his client's comment.

"Ron, I could see myself living here. What do you think?"

Winston smiled and looked Emma straight in the eye. "Well, Emma. It meets most of the criteria you mentioned," he said smiling. "And believe it or not, based on neighborhood statistics, crime is low here. There's also a small grocery store less than one block away, a library two streets over and mass transit at the corner. Plus, it's a one-level, just like you wanted. So I could see you living here, too. But whatever you want, Emma. That's the main thing."

Winston's nonchalance was well-placed and he wrote a full price offer for his client on the spot. Perhaps the nicest part of all was Emma's comment that she now wanted Winston to sell her old home, the one he'd sold her so many years earlier. Leaving the condo with Emma, Winston remained cautious.

Approaching the Saab, he carefully studied the back seat of his car for visitors, then looked underneath the vehicle just to be sure. On their trip to drop Emma off, Winston drove past the spot where he'd dumped his attacker an hour or so earlier. "Gone," Winston breathed.

"Good riddance," he thought. Minutes later, Winston had his client back to her place.

"Thanks so much, Ron, for helping me find such a nice house. I hope they accept my offer. You'll let me know right away?"

"Of course, Emma. I'll call you as soon as I receive a response."

Later that evening, as the acceptance of Emma's offer spat from Winston's home office printer, he decided to follow up a hunch...with a few questions of his own.

Chapter V

Legally Brief

Wide awake at 6:00 AM, Ron Winston hadn't slept much. He threw off the covers and ambled downstairs for breakfast. Hitting a few switches in the kitchen, soft jazz commenced while muted fluorescent lighting nudged him into consciousness. Bleary-eyed as the coffee maker began to gurgle, he buttered a bagel and continued to wake. "What will Dennis make of everything that's been going on?" Winston wondered aloud. Munching silently, he poured a cup of coffee, slipped in some cream and savored the aroma.

Winston showered, shaved, then splashed on his signature cologne and inhaled the spicy fragrance. He wore his standard, relaxed business attire: White shirt, chinos, black shoes, Brooks Brothers tie and a dark blue blazer. After a short stop at his office, by 9:30 AM Winston returned to his car and began to drive. Looking in his rear-view mirror, he recognized the same plain-looking sedan parked earlier that morning across the street from his house. "Great. Just great...they're still tailing me." Weaving in and out of traffic, it took a series of sharp turns before Winston felt safe. Twenty minutes later, he exited his vehicle with a deep breath. He began his brief walk from a large parking garage. As he looked up to grey skies, Winston breathed a prayer.

Once inside an adjacent building, he punched the button for a short elevator ride. The doors opened and Winston took a right turn toward the law office entrance of Dennis Worth, P.C. He walked past the front credenza and into the tastefully-appointed law office. Peering from behind his desk, the attorney was surprised to see his unannounced client.

"Ron…good to see you again."

Worth extended his gold cuff-linked hand. With a single shake, he motioned his guest to take a seat on the nearby plush leather couch. Sitting forward on his blood-red swivel chair with framed degrees behind him, Worth placed both hands flat on his dark oak desk.

"Talk to me about what happened to you yesterday."

"The guy just came out of nowhere, Dennis. If it had been a random robbery, I could probably handle it better. But I'm certain what he wanted was the film. He said 'You know what I'm here for.' Talk about terrifying."

Seeing Winston's palpable concerns, Worth mulled over the situation. "Given the evidence you now possess, Ron, you may very well be right about this. And whoever he is, this guy appears to be serious. So while the one who attacked you is likely long gone, to be frank, there may be others. We can't let this happen again. So there's now an argument to be made for getting you police protection. But that means we'll need to disclose the film to law enforcement before we can confirm what we have…plus, we really need to nail down your ownership, or you could conceivably lose all rights to the film in court."

Worth pulled his eyeglasses off and placed them on his desk. "I'll do whatever you want here, Ron. But if we ask for police protection, they'll have plenty of questions of their own and we'd better be ready to answer them. Decide on that, before we take the option of reporting to authorities any further. Because other than encouraging you to exercise your Fifth Amendment right to avoid self-incrimination, there may not be much else I can do. Maybe not even a plea deal, if they really get ticked-off. This then becomes more of an international affair and I'm only a Texas attorney."

Ron Winston nodded.

"You understand all that, Ron?"

Rubbing his temples, Winston tried to think.

"Ron, did anyone follow you up here?"

Winston shrugged his shoulders.

"How would I know, Dennis? I'm a real estate agent, remember? I LIKE it when people approach me. That is, until now."

Worth looked with pity at his client. "Let's shift gears. Since forensics may show the film could provide new information on the Kennedy assassination, we need to address some other things as well."

"What's that, Dennis?"

"The film's ownership. I want to get away from any kind of 'finders keepers' defense, if possible. That can make for a weak case, and juries tend to dislike any

85

hint of misappropriated property. You said the former homeowners where you found the film willingly relinquished it?"

"That's right."

"What's your evidence?"

"Their real estate agent told me. She said the sellers didn't want anything else in the house once they moved out."

Worth sighed. "I'd feel better if we could prove that, in case it ever comes up."

"Any ideas?"

"A few. But first, I'd like to know a little more about the former owners. Kind of a thumbnail psychological profile, in the event they ever raise a fuss. I want to think a few steps ahead of any high-powered lawyer they might bring in to claim rights to the film. Short of a signed statement, we'll want to document the conversation you had with the seller's agent who said the former owners 'didn't want anything else in the house.'"

Winston shrugged. "Sure. Whatever you say, Dennis."

"At some point, I'll want to depose the seller's agent, but that can come later. For now, write up a memo of what was said at the time you were told you could take the camera. Then we'll have you sign and date it with our notary."

Worth began punctuating every few words with a tap on his ample desk. "One other thing, Ron. Assuming they're still alive, see if you can find out where the former owners of the home now live. Whoever owned that house in 1963, they're possibly the ones who initially placed that camera in the attic. If necessary, you might want to order a chain of title search from one of the real estate escrow firms you do business with. That'll help us confirm who owned the house from November 22, 1963 onward. At that point we can find out who they are, about any potential weaknesses and craft a logical case for your ownership of the film."

"Anything else, Dennis?"

"Keeping this low-key would be best. In speaking with the former camera owners, you might want to frame it in a pleasant manner by letting them know your buyers absolutely love their old house, but have a few questions. Disclose as little as possible about the camera. Maybe intimate the new owners want to remodel."

"Oh, like ask the former owners if they know a certain wall might be weight-bearing?"

"Right. That kind of thing. If you can, befriend them. Build a relationship and some trust. I could do it, but you real estate agents are better at that kind of schmoozing thing. Besides, having you do it is more logical and natural. It also frees me up to research the more arcane legal minefields. You might try bantering with their agent first."

Winston shifted in his seat. "That could be tricky, Dennis."

"Tricky? Why?" Worth looked quizzical.

Winston looked out the window, off into the distance. "Because real estate salespeople can get very territorial about other agents talking with their clients, even those from years ago."

Worth was unfazed. "Well, I think it's worth giving a shot, but you know your business better than I do. Maybe buy their agent lunch. That seems ethical enough. Present company excluded, I've long noticed that real estate agents tend to be chow hounds."

Winston laughed. "Touche´, Dennis."

"So, Ron…feel things out. Just don't reveal anything that's happening on this end. Simply imply that your clients may want to get in touch with the former owners sometime to discuss the house. And make sure to document the time and date you speak with anyone and precisely what was said. Whatever you do, don't tip your hand, and call me if you have any questions."

"Got it. Thanks, Dennis. If I ever got the former owners to sign off on my keeping the camera and contents, that'd be the biggest sale I've ever made."

Winston's mission was now clear. Find and convince people he'd never met to relinquish all rights to one of the most highly-sought treasures in U.S. history: New photographic evidence on the assassination of President John F. Kennedy. Winston got right to work the very next day. After ordering and reviewing several documents, he grabbed the phone, talking points in hand.

"Hi Sheila—Ron at Lone Star Realty."

"Hi Ron. I haven't spoken with you for a while. Are your buyers still excited about the house they bought?"

"Sure are. They love it. Say, by the way, I do have one question, though."

There was a pause at the other end of the phone. "What's that? Do your buyers have a problem?"

"No, we're in luck with my folks," Winston chuckled. "But the chain of title shows your sellers bought the property in 1976."

Sheila laughed. "Do you order a chain of title often?"

"Oh, occasionally. Mainly for lawsuit protection."

"You know, that's not a bad idea. Maybe I should be doing that, too."

"If you had our scary errors & omissions insurance coverage, you'd be doing it already. Anyway, I was wondering...did you happen to know the folks who sold the house to *your* sellers?"

"Sure did—the Maxwell's. That was my first year in the business."

As Sheila spoke, Winston began scribbling every piece of information he heard. "Sara kept an immaculate house," she continued. "I never gave it the 'white glove' test, but remember thinking it was so spotless you could have eaten off the floor. As for myself, I remember trying so hard to do everything right. I also 'double-dipped' that particular transaction. Since I was on both sides of the deal, it was a great paycheck. Even bought a car with the commission. But why do you ask?"

"Well since it sounds like the Maxwell's are the ones who owned the house early on, my buyers might want to talk with them sometime and learn more about the home they just bought. Stuff like possible blueprints, weight-bearing walls, that kind of thing."

"I heard Bill Maxwell passed away a while back. Sara should be helpful, but she was in quite a bit of pain when they sold it."

"Pain?"

"As I recall, they lost their son Teddy several years before selling. That's when I first met Sara—at church, looking for answers. In fact, she was in my Bible study class for awhile. Then I moved clear across town. A few years after I sold her and Bill's house, I think she may have moved again. I haven't seen her in years. I hope she found her answers, though; she's really a sweet person."

"Thanks, Sheila and I really appreciate all your help on the transaction. I hope you didn't spend your paycheck the first day you got it."

"Not quite—it lasted nearly a week! Thank you for having such strong buyers."

There was now one big item on Winston's 'to-do' list: Meet Sara Maxwell. A few days later on a sunny Saturday morning, Winston lolled inside his den, clad in his most comfortable jeans, sweatshirt and athletic socks. Armed with a name, Winston realized he might only have one good shot in befriending Sara Maxwell. He could not misstep in approaching the likely former owner of the film he now held, and considered his options aloud.

"I need to do some groundwork and find out what she's like. Once I review the tax database, hopefully I can track her address down. But a plausible meeting…that *is* a problem. Maybe I can arrange to just bump into her somehow. Since Sheila seems okay with it, there should be no surprise when I speak with Sara Maxwell about a house she sold decades ago. I could mention that Sheila gave me her name. But then maybe it'd be too weird for me to come right out and start asking someone about a house they sold so long ago. She might think I'm an identity thief, or some kind of scammer."

For hours, Winston ran every scenario he could think of through his mind. "Let's see. Walk past her yard and strike up a conversation about, oh, I don't know…bird-watching. Only problem is, I don't bird-watch."

Feeling desperate, he narrowed his choices. "Maybe call her and say I'm selling siding…*or houses*." Winston clapped his hands together and reminded himself: "I've already *got* the perfect cover. Tell her the truth…I SELL HOUSES FOR A LIVING. But I can't start out with that. I need to play dumb and somehow steer the conversation to her old house. Then the coincidence that I sold it could just happen."

Winston eventually realized that no matter how strong of a coincidence he contrived, he simply didn't have it in him to attempt pulling off such a fishy tale.

"Better to play it straight. Tell Sara Maxwell that I represented the current owners and simply hope for some information on the house. Then parlay from there into a discussion about the found camera. Make it an 'Oh, by the way' kind of thing. That seems far more believable and I'm not going to lie."

Armed now with a credible strategy of how to meet Sara Maxwell, Winston began assembling background information to find the common ground necessary to quickly place their meeting on a positive note and help establish a relationship. Hopefully, the house they had in common would be enough. But Winston realized that knowing Sara's likes and dislikes could help increase his 'friendliness quotient' and thereby positively influence the conversation. He thought long and hard.

"Not much on the Internet about Sara and Bill Maxwell, or their son Theodore. Maybe the library."

Approaching the main Dallas library, Winston took a deep breath. "Where to start?" he asked himself. Through the doors waited his answer in the form of the library's information desk. Winston began asking questions of a matronly librarian.

"Hi, I'm researching information on area residents. Is there some kind of catalogue for locating information about them, stuff like news stories and obituaries?"

Looking up, the gray-haired woman tugged on a metal eyeglass chain looped around her neck. "We have. One place to start is in the newspaper archive index upstairs. But if you're pretty sure the person is deceased, you might want to first try the SSDI, or social security death index in the computer section downstairs."

"I'm pretty sure he's deceased."

"Then definitely try the SSDI," the librarian stated emphatically in her distinctly Southern accent. That'll give you a good way to narrow the dates. From there, you can more easily search through local newspapers."

"Then what?"

"Once you have a name and time frame, I'd suggest searching the newspaper index located upstairs. Particularly good is the Dallas Morning News. It's been in continuous circulation since 1885 and our records go back nearly as far. Definitely go there after you try the SSDI."

"Thanks."

Winston descended deep into the old library. With plenty of available computers to choose from, he wandered to the back row. Typing the name 'Theodore Maxwell' into the social security death index yielded dozens of names, but only three looked like they died as

young men from Texas. Scribbling down the three dates
of death, Winston ambled over to a vast series of
microfilm files.

"The Dallas Morning News *does* seem like a good
place to start," Winston reasoned. He scrolled through
obituary sections of the newspaper from three different
microfilm spools, using approximate dates from the
SSDI. On the third try he whispered "Paydirt." A
moment later, he mouthed the words on the screen before
him: "Theodore Richard Maxwell, son of Bill & Sara
Maxwell. Killed in action in Vietnam during combat.
Posthumously awarded the Purple Heart and Bronze Star.
Services pending."

"That's him," Winston thought. "Only 19 years
old." Winston hit the 'print' button. As the machine
hummed, he glanced above the obituary to a news article
titled 'Dallas Hero Returns Home.'

From   Wire   Reports   –   The
remains   of   a   local   army
private   were   delivered   to
military   officials   in   Dallas
for   internment   later   this
week. PFC Theodore R. 'Teddy'
Maxwell was killed 6 days ago
when he was ambushed by North
Vietnamese   fire.   Maxwell
joined the Army in 1974 and
had   been   stationed   near
Saigon   for   several   months
before   his   death.   He   is
survived by his parents Bill

& Sara Maxwell. The family
suggests contributions be
made to the Boy Scouts.

Helped by this piece of confirming data, Winston
still had a problem. He had yet to find Teddy Maxwell's
mother, someone he'd never met, who may no longer
even be alive. Winston headed back to his home office.
Tapping a pencil on his desk in steady cadence, he felt
stymied.

Normally, his real estate research skills readily
yielded any information needed, but no Sara Maxwell
was identified as a residential property owner in the
Dallas Metroplex. "Lots of S. Maxwell's, but that could
stand for Sam, Steve, or even Sylvester," Winston
reasoned. "Worst of all, she could be living pretty much
anywhere by now, assuming she's still living."

Winston began to methodically analyze the
challenge before him. "If she's still alive, she's could be
re-married and living under another name, renting an
apartment...or in assisted living." Seated in front of his
home computer later that Saturday afternoon, he
wondered aloud: "Where to start?" Winston began with
a few Internet search engines. Entering the name Sara
Maxwell in an online Dallas phone directory, he tried to
look at the bright side and reminded himself: "At least
it's not a name like Mary Smith." Ten minutes of
searching later, he threw a bent paper clip at the nearby
garbage can.

"Nothing. How about Sarah Maxwell," Winston
asked himself. His fingers clattered on the keyboard, yet

the screen offered little. "No dice there, either." He sighed. "Maybe she remarried. This could be tricky." He swallowed hard. "How about the SSDI? It worked for their son." That shrinking sliver of a possibility could discern if his quarry was even still alive. "Snake eyes on that one...whew," he sighed. "At least I don't have to abandon all hope."

With further searching, Winston had a bead on several distinct possibilities. Through a combination of Internet sources he determined that ninety seven S. Maxwell's resided in Texas, with eleven in the Dallas Metroplex. He then matched one of them with the address of three S. Maxwell's using his real estate agent tax database from the local multiple listing system. Only one phone number matched. Once the name and phone number were printed, he grabbed the phone before he lost his nerve. After several rings, an elderly woman's voice replied.

"Hello?"

"Hi—my name is Ron and I'm a real estate agent. I'm calling to find if you happened to sell a home on the 500 block of Parkhurst Drive around 1976?"

There was a pause.

"Who did you say you were?"

"Ron Winston, real estate agent with Lone Star Realty."

"Why yes, we sold a home there around then. Is something wrong?"

"No, not at all. As a matter of fact, several months ago I sold it to buyer clients of mine and they absolutely love it. Paperwork in the chain of title shows the home was probably built by you and your husband. I was just calling to see if we could meet to talk about the house. I'd like to take some notes and tell the new owners about details of their new home that aren't readily apparent."

"Is this common? To call people so long after they sold their house?"

Winston let out a well-timed 'Tsk.'

"Sadly, at most real estate firms, it isn't common at all. But at our firm, it is. We provide high quality service to our clients, long after the sale."

Winston next went for what sales professionals call the 'assumptive close.' "How does Friday morning around nine sound? Can I stop by then?"

Softening, Sara replied with "I suppose so." Then her voice turned wistful. "Do you have any pictures of the house now?"

"Why yes, I do. One from the multiple listing system and a few I took myself. I'll bring them with me."

"How nice. That house still holds so many memories. Our son grew up there. Of course, I don't go out much anymore."

Winston remained focused. "I understand. When I stop by Friday I'll show them to you. Are you at 332 Arlington Way?"

"Yes, I am. You have that information about me, too?"

Winston laughed. "Tax records make my life a lot easier. Don't worry, though. Real estate agents go through a criminal background check. They fingerprint us and our mug shots are in the hands of authorities, so you're in safe hands. Thank you again for your time today. I'll see you on Friday."

"Goodbye."

Moments later, Winston phoned his attorney.

"Dennis, I have the appointment."

"With the film's likely former owner?"

"Sure do. This Friday."

"I'll give you a release for her to sign. If for some reason she won't sign it, we still have several legal avenues to pursue. But it will be easier if she agrees, especially before news of this gets out. People—even little old ladies—can get greedy once the press breaks a story like this."

Friday came quickly. After some additional coaching from Dennis, Winston was ready. He decided to play it loose and rose at 5:45 AM to give himself plenty of time. He took a morning walk, ate a bagel with lox and sipped coffee while reading the paper, all the while reminding himself not to be late. Several hours later, he pulled out of his garage and began the drive to the upscale North Dallas suburb of Highland Park. Before leaving his car, Winston smiled in his rear view mirror, adjusted his necktie and sighed "Here goes."

He approached the stately colonial style home located in the toniest of Texas neighborhoods. Appreciating the home's charming dormers, Winston fantasized about the commissions. *I'll have to start 'farming' this area for business*, he mentally noted. *I'd love to sell some houses here.*

Moments later, he knocked on the simple red door featuring a gold plaque with the name 'Maxwell.' A small dog barked. What came next sounded like heeled shoes across a wooden floor.

"Hello. You must be Ron," said the woman extending her hand.

"I am," he replied with a gentle handshake. "You must be Sara. I can already tell you have a lovely house. Hope you don't mind…Since I'm a real estate agent, I feel entitled to comment."

"Why of course. Thank you. Please come in."

She placed her small, now-yapping dog in an adjacent room. Nervously flitting about and sporting a dowager's hump, Sara Maxwell looked pretty much like Winston expected: A nice older lady who now lived alone.

"Can I get you something to drink; coffee or iced tea?"

"Oh, coffee please."

"I'll be right back. Please make yourself comfortable."

Taking his seat on a plush pale yellow sofa, Winston glanced about the room. Family portraits surrounded him. Craning his neck, he noticed a series of one boy's photos in progression. Beginning at birth, they continued through high school graduation and into the military. His host returned with two steaming cups of coffee. Winston waited until she finished placing them on drink coasters and sat down.

"Is that your son?"

"Yes. He passed away in 1974. In Vietnam. He was just 19."

"I'm very sorry."

"Every day I think about Teddy. His father and I just adored him. Now both he and his Dad are in a better place. Do you have children?"

"No...but lots of nieces and nephews," Winston hurriedly responded.

"Love them while you can."

After an awkward pause, Sara Maxwell pulled a roll of paper from the large brown bag beside her.

"Bill and I had very clear ideas about the house we would build. Everything we'd seen back then was so 'cookie-cutter.' We were after something different. After you called, I looked and found these right where I stored them after we moved."

She handed Winston a large roll of blueprints.

"Your people can have them if they'd like. Hopefully they'll be useful. I won't be needing them anymore."

"Why thank you," Winston said as he unfurled the outer roll to take a peek. "You're very kind. I know my clients will appreciate these. If they decide to add on or remodel, planning will be easier by knowing which walls are weight-bearing and where the studs are."

"Bill would have helped you a lot more than I ever could, but hopefully those will help." With hands folded in her lap, Sara Maxwell's face grew hopeful. "Did you mention you had photos of our old place?"

"Oh, I almost forgot. Yes—right here."

Winston padded his blue blazer and reached inside, extracting a long envelope from his breast pocket.

"Here they are."

He splayed six photos of the former Maxwell house on the coffee table before them.

"Here's a photo of the exterior. I printed that one from the multiple listing system. That's how I found your old house was for sale, before showing it to my buyer clients."

As Sara bent closer to the table, her head began to nod slightly. Winston sensed it might be some kind of a palsy-like condition. She suddenly brightened.

"Oh, it still looks a lot like when we lived there." Pointing a bony finger at one exterior photo, she remarked: "The maple tree has really grown, too. It couldn't have been two feet high when we planted it."

Sara looked up. "I haven't been by in so long."

"You should stop by sometime, Winston replied. "I know my buyers would love to meet you." Winston pointed at several other photos. "These are the ones I took just a few weeks ago of the interior after they did some painting. Here's a picture of the kitchen, the dining area and one of the living room."

Sara smiled. "I like what they've done. Even though I might have used different colors, it looks like your clients retained a sense of classic design. There aren't any far-out combinations."

Ever the salesperson, Winston reminded himself to mentally file away a snapshot of Sara's personality. *This lady really has style,* he thought. *And she knows what she likes, that's for sure.*

"Well, the new owners might make some changes toward a more traditional look, once they're settled in," Winston said. "They asked me to recommend someone to help them, but I don't know anyone good with traditional interior designs."

Sara grew animated and pointed one finger toward the floor.

"I know *just* the person. She helped us here."

"No kidding? If you have a name or company I'll pass it along."

Winston sensed the breaking of his host's reserved façade. Sara began to laugh and clapped her hands.

"Flo Mo. Florence Moriarity...in case you couldn't guess, she's Irish. Friends and customers call her Flo Mo. I think her company is called Designers West. I've got her card somewhere."

Winston smiled. "That's a name even I can remember. I'll tell my clients to ask for 'Flo Mo' at Designers West. And Sara, if you'd like to keep the photos, they're yours; I've made copies."

"Really? Thank you! I have a box around here I keep my photos in. Are you sure?"

Her comment jostled Winston's memory of why he was even there. "Absolutely. Say, speaking of boxes, I was going to ask *you* a favor."

"What's that?"

"During the home inspection a few months ago, a few old boxes turned up. If you don't mind, we have a standard release form for previous owners to sign, simply to ensure that any disposal of contents from a house is completely above-board."

Sara Maxwell paused. "Did the boxes contain anything?"

"Come to think of it, some chewed up newspapers and an old, beat-up camera.

Sara looked hopefully at Winston. "A camera. Really? In our old house?"

"Yeah, it's hard to say what the deal was with it," Winston said. "I don't know much about them, myself. If any family photos were ever found in it, I'm sure we could send you copies. Of course, it's been so long." Winston bit his tongue for a moment. "Anyway, it's a standard release form, if you don't mind signing it."

Sara Maxwell picked up the release with both hands. Pulling it close to her face, she began to read aloud. "The undersigned hereby releases any and all ownership interest(s) in any and all contents from their former residence at 511 Parkhurst Drive, Dallas, Texas."

"Well, I don't know why not," Sara said as if to convince herself. "You've been so nice to me and all. Besides, I don't suppose much would last in an attic after all this time, do you?"

"Probably not…but if something about your family ever turns up, I'll make sure to let you know." Winston took a deep breath as Sara picked up his Mont

Blanc pen, signed the document and handed both back to Winston. She looked up at him and smiled.

"I did a good job of cleaning that old house, I know that for sure. It took me nearly a week and that's when I was a lot younger, too." Sara turned taciturn. "Would you let me know if you or the new owners find any of my son's things? He meant the world to me."

"Absolutely," Winston said reassuringly. "In fact, let me make a note of it," he boomed while scribbling ostentatiously in large swooping motions on his yellow notepad. Winston desperately wanted to change the subject—and fast.

"I really appreciate your telling me about Flo Mo. As a real estate agent, I know many of my clients could sure use her services."

"If you talk with her, please tell her Sara says 'Hi.'"

"Will do."

Winston slid the now-signed release in his file and stood up. "Thanks again, Sara. I'll send you remodel photos when my buyers finish their decorating. Or if you're up to it, maybe we could arrange a tour of your old place."

"That would be lovely."

Winston's feet didn't touch the ground all the way out to his car. Later in the day, he checked into his attorney's office. They shook hands and sat down.

"Good to see you, Ron. Any word yet on your info-gathering exploits?"

"Got everything we need."

"Whoa. Good work. Do you have it with you?"

"Right here."

Reviewing the document, Worth smiled. "You weren't kidding—everything we need, indeed. This is going to be very helpful." Worth rose from behind his desk and took a deep breath. "Ron, I think we should shift gears again."

"How so, Dennis?"

"Before we're slapped with a subpoena to surrender your evidence, I'd like to be the one to choose the time and place…while we still can. When one deals with the United States government, there's a lot to be said for taking any opportunity to influence the outcome."

"What do you have in mind?"

"A phone call."

"Sounds reasonable. Who?"

"The FBI at first. Then possibly the CIA. At the moment, I hope to play one side against the other with a fair degree of effectiveness."

"Whatever you think, Dennis. I'm a businessman, not an expert on intelligence agencies."

Winston watched as his attorney picked up the phone and dialed. "Hello? This is attorney Dennis Worth. Is Deputy Director Sabino available? Thank you; I'll hold." Worth cupped his hand over the phone and whispered across his desk.

"It may be a few minutes, but I'd rather not play phone tag with this guy. He's *very* hard to reach."

Winston nodded in agreement. Moments later, Worth raised his eyebrows.

"Yes, Mr. Director. Thank you for taking my call. I promise to be brief. As I mentioned to one of your aides, my client has acquired—through legal means— evidence of potential interest to the bureau." There was a long pause. "You were told correctly...*John F.* Kennedy. Since I am an officer of the court, my hope is that we can discuss the transfer of evidence to your custody, without delay. In exchange, we merely request your assistance in defense of our ownership rights if needed, and a copyright non-infringement agreement. I'm sure we can reach an understanding."

The expectant look on Dennis' face turned to a frown.

"I'm sorry to hear that. My hope was to work with the bureau instead of the CIA. My client and I can go either way, or perhaps to the media...but we'd prefer to work with you, Mr. Director, if at all possible."

Worth's eyebrows rose. For nearly a minute he listened and gradually broke a smile. "I'd like that too, Mr. Sabino. We'll wait for your call here at my office tomorrow morning. Ten would be fine. Thank you again."

Worth exhaled deeply and looked up at Winston.

"I'm glad we at least got their attention. When I mentioned the CIA, he changed his attitude in a hurry. They know we could present our case to several government agencies and the FBI doesn't want others, particularly the media, delving into any of their possible mistakes that might be spun differently."

Winston smiled. "So that's how it works…good cop, bad cop. Even when dealing with cops."

"Darn right," Dennis replied. "For us, one distinct advantage is that the FBI would probably be a lot more predictable to deal with, at least compared to the CIA."

Tapping the desk with his eyeglasses, Worth continued dispassionately, even robot-like. "Sure, the FBI can play rough…and their morass of rules is confounding at times…but the bureau is generally a bunch of straight-shooters. They're really law-and-order guys…and gals."

Worth looked up at Winston candidly. "Plus, I'd rather not worry about either of us being exiled to a little-known foreign country for interrogation." The mere thought of languishing in some rogue nation's prison had Winston readily agreeing.

At precisely 10 AM the following morning, Winston sat in attorney Dennis Worth's office. A single beep sounded, as a disembodied female voice on a phone speaker interrupted their discussion.

"Mr. Worth—It sounds like a priority call for you on line two."

"Thanks, Sherry," Worth said and calmly picked up the phone.

"Hello, Dennis Worth."

Worth paused, then began to speak. "You're already here? Then come on up."

After another pause, Worth seemed taken aback.

"Could you please hold for a moment?"

He pressed the phone's hold button, set the phone down and looked across his desk at Winston.

"It's the FBI. They want to discuss this in *their* offices, right away."

"How soon is right away?"

"There's a car waiting downstairs."

Palms turned skyward, Winston shot his attorney an unknowing glance. "What do you think, Dennis?"

"We can try to prolong this, Ron. But sooner or later, they *will* have the opportunity to ask questions and they're pretty anxious right now. If they're that gung-ho to taxi us to them, maybe they brought people in overnight to deal with this. Otherwise, if it's so important, why didn't they handle this yesterday?"

"Whatever you suggest. I don't have any appointments today that can't be rescheduled."

Worth cleared his throat and picked up the phone.

"Thanks for holding. We'll be down in five minutes."

Rising up to go downstairs, Worth looked calmly at Winston.

"Ron, if you're unsure about anything they ask, defer to me. Take the fifth if you have to, but don't be intimidated. We'll get through this."

Out in the hallway, Winston queried: "How long *could* they hold us, Dennis?"

"It depends. I expect we'll be free to go after a brief meeting."

As Worth and Winston left the elevator, two men in suits and sunglasses appeared out of nowhere.

"Mr. Winston, Mr. Worth?"

In true salesperson fashion, Winston reflexively extended his hand to the nearest man. "Ron Winston—pleased to meet you." Pointing to the exit door, the man's response was classic government monotone.

"This way, please."

As the four approached the parking lot, a long, dark blue limousine approached. Winston was struck by a similarity to the president's vehicle in Dallas on

November 22nd, 1963. His attorney was obviously thinking the same thing, since he whispered in agreement: "The only thing missing are flags on the hood."

Their escorts circled the car and opened both rear doors.

"Have a seat."

The doors slammed shut and an eerie quiet consumed the vehicle. After a few minutes of downtown traffic, the ride was mostly freeway. Looking around inside the vehicle, Winston noticed there were no door handles. He peered out the virtually black tinted windows and wondered what he'd tell his fiance'. Worth looked helplessly over to his client and said nothing, certain the limo was bugged.

Less than half an hour later, the car slowed, then abruptly halted. The car doors opened a block or so away from a tall building of marble and glass. Leaning toward the car was a beefy man with military bearing. He had a shaved head and a semi-automatic pistol holstered on his hip. An earpiece was attached to his dark sunglasses.

"Identification?"

As if in a movie, the FBI escorts flipped open their wallets. "These two are with us."

Turning to Winston and Worth, the order from the man with the shaved head was simple. "Follow me, please." The FBI men accompanying them each checked their heretofore hidden handguns at the entrance. After a series of metal detectors and wand waving in a side room, Winston, Worth and their escorts stood before a wall of elevators next to a waiting attendant.

"Fourteen, please." The group piled in. Moments later, doors opened to a dark paneled anteroom. On the receptionist's desk was a sign that read **Office of Deputy Bureau Director**.

"We've scheduled a meeting for now."

"He's cleared his morning appointments to see you. I'll buzz you in."

Moments later, the four men entered a large, well-appointed room. In one corner was a fully enclosed glass cubicle with a large oval table and half a dozen chairs. Winston guessed it was some kind of portable soundproof room. Inside sat the Southwest region's most powerful federal law enforcement officer. Winston had a nice view from a large window. Winston and Worth were guided by the FBI men, and all four walked into the glass cubicle. Reading a file, the man behind the table didn't stand or shake hands with anyone. He simply looked up and spoke slowly.

"I'm Deputy Bureau Director Sabino. Would you mind taking a seat and please introduce yourself?"

"I'm attorney Dennis Worth, representing my client Ron Winston."

Hands now folded on the desk before him, Sabino smiled unconvincingly. "Pleased to meet you, but forgive me while I cut to the chase. I understand you've taken possession of criminal evidence and from not just any crime. Where is it?"

Worth spoke calmly. "Mr. Director, I've discussed this with my client and we're very willing to provide to you what could be evidence. My client will comply in good faith with all legal requirements for a smooth transfer of custody. However, we're requesting two things. A written agreement and time."

Sabino's flabby jowls turned taut as he paused. Standing up, he walked around his desk to a window overlooking the city. After what seemed like several minutes, he crossed his arms and began to fidget. Tapping a finger against his crossed arms, the director continued staring from the window. Finally, he spoke.

"You say you need time. What kind of time? Tonight?"

Worth responded in a respectful tone. "Actually, sir, we can guarantee delivery to you within 10 days, probably less."

The director turned around and walked toward the two men. Out of nowhere Sabino slammed his hand in a single concussive motion on the desk between them. Veins popping on his forehead, the deputy director's formerly pale face suddenly resembled a red cabbage. Sabino looked downward and directly in front of the seated attorney.

"TEN DAYS? Tell you what I'm going to do, counselor. You have *precisely* 72 hours from this exact moment to physically deliver any and all evidence you have to this office. One *minute* later and I'll have a warrant issued for *both* of your arrests. In the meanwhile, you're both to surrender your passports and submit to monitoring bracelets. We're talking a capital crime of global significance, gentlemen, and I'm not playing games. Do I make myself clear to you and your client, counselor?"

Worth was more solemn than Winston had ever witnessed.

"Yes sir, Mr. Sabino. May I ask one other question, sir?"

"What is it?" he grimaced.

Worth pulled a file from the briefcase between his legs and handed it across the desk.

"My client has legal standing to lay claim as the property's owner. Prior to our delivery of the evidence, would you please review this agreement for copyright protection and return of the film?"

"You people just don't give up, do you?" Sabino grimaced at Worth, then shrugged.

"No guarantees, but I'll have Pemberton, our lead counsel, review it and get back to you upon our receiving the evidence."

Worth nodded his head ostentatiously. "Thank you, sir."

A door knock elicited "Come in" from the director's assistant. Two young men dressed in what appeared to be guard uniforms entered. Each carried a rubber-band like device with a domino-looking attachment.

"Gentlemen, these are your monitoring bracelets. To illustrate my beneficence while saving you unnecessary embarrassment and prying questions, we'll place them on your ankles as long as you behave. If you don't behave, we can have them re-fitted for your wrist, neck, or you can guess what other body parts we might try strapping them onto."

Winston instinctively winced whilst drawing his knees together. After a few minutes, the bracelets were in place. Sabino cleared his throat.

"Your passports are to be surrendered by 6:00 PM today."

As the two men were leaving the room, Sabino's voice reverberated one final time.

"71 hours, twenty eight minutes and counting, counselor."

Winston and Worth said nothing as they were escorted outside to their waiting limousine. Arriving back at Worth's office, the exiting vehicle drove off before either uttered a word.

Winston spoke first. "What's next, Dennis?"

"I've got plenty of ideas," Worth replied in a hushed tone. "But our next move depends on what you want to accomplish. Let's go up to my office."

Back inside Worth's law office, the two men plopped down on waiting leather chairs.

"What do you mean, our next move depends on what I want? Surrendering the tape is optional?"

"Sure it is, at least for now. But a delay could get nasty...and expensive. All the feds need to do is claim a 'national security' interest. They could then put out a 'gag order,' along with a court-approved seal on all documents and slap subpoenas on both of us. That would also give us the disadvantage of preventing our pressuring the government with media coverage, which is what I'd normally attempt to ensure the feds play fair."

"So we give them the film?"

"Either that, Ron, or we convince them that it's in their best interests to play nice."

"Dennis. I realize you're the legal mind here. But I have to wonder—since this *is* the same US government that brought us the IRS. How could you *possibly* get 'the feds,' as you call them, to play nice?"

A smile erupted from his attorney's face. "I've known...and worked with *lots* of government employees. In fact, I was one myself, right out of law school and even taught a course for government employees during my time as a county prosecutor. So I know a bit about what I'm saying. What you have to understand about *any* government operation is that there is *always* a hierarchy...a 'pecking order,' if you will."

"Alright. Fine. Makes sense."

"So the secret, Ron, to getting anything done in a 'pecking order' system…is that if you're getting nowhere, always go *up* the chain of command. Never down."

"Fine, Dennis. That's all very well and good. But what does that MEAN?"

"Deputy director Sabino is no doubt loyal to the FBI. But if we can convince him that it's in his best interest to work with us in a win-win manner, that's where we start."

"And if we can't convince him?"

"Then we go up the chain of command."

"Okay, that makes sense. A principal rule of sales is to never ask someone who can't say 'yes.'"

"Exactly. Besides, Ron…as powerful as he appears, he's still only a deputy."

"Only a deputy," Winston nodded. "So where does that leave us? I mean, who's higher than a deputy?"

"Well the director himself. He's in Washington, D.C."

Worth walked to his wall of books and pulled out a volume. "Here it is. Law Enforcement Agencies of the United States." After a minute thumbing through the directory, Dennis Worth looked up at Winston. "He's in here."

"Whaddya think then, Dennis?"

"I realize it's a long shot…but at this point, I really don't think we have a lot to lose…that is, unless you want to try the CIA."

Looking across the room at one another, Winston and Worth each hesitated for a moment. In tandem, they shook their heads decidedly in the negative. Worth spoke next.

"That's what I thought. So I'll give the FBI director a try, then." Worth walked behind his desk, sat down and cleared his throat. Punching numbers on his telephone, he looked up at Winston. "It's ringing." There was a brief pause.

"Yes, Hello. This is attorney Dennis Worth in Dallas. Would it be possible for me to speak briefly with the director? I may have a legitimate lead on the JFK assassination." After a pause, Worth simply said "Certainly."

Worth cupped one hand over the telephone and smiled at Winston. "They're putting me through to his secretary." The wait wasn't long.

"Yes, hello. This is attorney Dennis Worth in Dallas. I was hoping to speak with the director. Actually, it's about the assassination of John F. Kennedy. Yes, that's right. Well, my main purpose for calling has to do with what appears to be my client's new-found evidence on the case. No, I don't believe the director is aware of this. Why yes, I'd be glad to hold."

Worth was patched through in less than one minute. "Yes, Mr. Director. I'm Dennis Worth, attorney with Worth and Associates in Dallas. Thank you for taking my call. Yes, that's right, John F. Kennedy. The evidence my client has involves newly-found movie footage of the assassination. Why yes, we were in touch here locally with Deputy Director Sabino. Unfortunately, that's the reason for my calling you. Well, I said unfortunately because he came off a bit inflexible and well, quite frankly…ham-fisted."

Worth nodded and listened for a several minutes. "I was wondering if perhaps we could deal with your office, instead of Mr. Sabino, to arrange for the transfer of evidence while safeguarding my client's proper ownership rights. That would be terrific. When would be a good time? I'm sure we can be available. Alright. I'll inform my client. We look forward to it. Thank you, sir."

Hanging up the phone, Worth was beaming. "He seemed extremely interested, Ron."

"How so?"

"Well, enough so that he wants to meet with us. Sabino may even have briefed him, so my phone call just now might not have been a surprise. I'm to call the director in the morning and arrange a time. Almost as important, it sounds like at least for now, Sabino is out of the picture. All I needed to mention was *new* evidence. I suspect the FBI head man will be a little more reasonable. That being the case, your rights to the film should be better respected than by whatever Sabino would have agreed to."

"You want to meet here in the morning to strategize, Ron?"

"You got it," Winston said.

"Fine, then. I'll see you here at 8 AM. Sharp. Just make sure you get plenty of sleep. In this meeting, they won't necessarily be interrogating you, but they *will* ask a lot of questions. It'll help if you're fresh."

Winston stood up and shook Worth's hand.

"Thanks, Dennis. You're a pal. And a dang fine attorney."

As Winston exited the room Dennis hollered "See you at 8 AM. And don't mess with that ankle bracelet in the meanwhile!"

Winston's alarm clock was obnoxiously loud at 5:30 AM. Knowing he could use some morning exercise to loosen up for the day ahead, he threw on his jogging clothes. In minutes he was pounding pavement outside his home in the Dallas suburbs. Legs gaining momentum, he immediately relaxed. Winston began to zone-out sufficiently to put his now-crazy life behind him.

Back home half an hour later with his head cleared, he hit the shower, shaved, got dressed and drove off with plenty of time for breakfast along the way. Exiting his car on what looked like a promising, sunny morning, Winston walked across the sparse restaurant parking lot. He pushed several coins into the newspaper machine and yanked one out of the metal box. Winston glanced at the headlines as he approached the entrance. *Ahhh*, he thought, falling into the window seat of a favorite morning haunt, Omelette Haven. The pert waitress didn't take long to pour him a glass of water.

"Coffee?"

"Sure. With the meal, please."

"What'll it be today?"

"Make it the Farmhand Breakfast."

"Bacon or sausage?"

"Both."

"Links or patties?"

"Let's try links this time."

"It'll just be a few minutes, Hon."

"Thanks."

Try as he might, it was difficult for Winston to concentrate on newspaper headlines. His mind churned, wondering what questions he'd be asked and how best to respond. He put the newspaper aside, then glanced out a nearby window wondering "Will they arrest me for holding criminal evidence? Will I lose my real estate license for taking what wasn't clearly mine, from a house bought by a client I represented?" After wolfing down breakfast, Winston arrived at his attorney's office just before 8 AM.

"Hey Ron. Good morning."

"Likewise, Dennis."

"I spoke with the FBI again, just a few minute ago."

"What'd they have to say?"

"Believe it or not, the director flew into DFW last night. We're to meet him at their Dallas office in about an hour."

"You're kidding, right?"

"No, I'm not kidding. He clearly has a sense of how turned off we were by his deputy director here. My comments about Sabino's bedside manner weren't the first he'd heard, either."

The drive into downtown Dallas was brief, but comfortable in Worth's late model Mercedes convertible.

"So, what's the worse-case scenario today, Dennis?"

"Worse-case? That's a tough one," Worth responded as he craned his neck to merge on the freeway.

"I suppose they could accuse us of impeding a federal investigation, or perhaps receiving stolen property. Neither is likely to stick, though, in my opinion."

Winston smiled. "That makes me feel a little bit better."

"But don't think they won't try to intimidate to get what they want," Worth warned.

"Terrific," Winston said. "So what's our strategy?"

"Number one, don't lie about anything."

"Anything else?"

"Number two, if in doubt, let me do the talking."

"Is there a number three?"

"Buy time until Randall Mackey can tell us more about the film."

"Any particular reason? I mean, the FBI has their own team of experts, right?"

Worth sighed. "Yes, they do. However, as Randall said, the FBI has been accused of 'doctoring' segments of evidence, including the Zapruder film involving this very same assassination. The copy we have has yet to even be placed in FBI hands. Therefore, given questions about what might later be considered 'tainted' evidence, some could consider our copy of the film to be more legitimate."

"Doctoring evidence...who'd ever think?"

"All conspiracy theories usually have some basis in fact, however remote. What I want to do is to maintain a 'control' version of the film so that if copies ever do get played with, we can verify what's known in legal circles as a legitimate 'chain of custody,' while preserving at least one original version of the film. That way, our original is less likely to be questioned."

"Keeping the government honest, huh?"

"That's part of it. But having researched this case as much as Mackey has, he noted that those outside of law enforcement can be every bit as reckless and damaging."

"How so?"

"For the sake of argument, let's first assume guilt is finally established. Then also for the sake of argument, let's say the guilty party ends up being affiliated with the Mob, the former Soviet Union, Cuba, or a myriad other groups. Next, imagine someone in that nefarious group either 'liquidating' those who hold new-found evidence, bribing them to get it, or otherwise tampering with it."

Worth sighed before continuing. "While it's unlikely that any more than a single rogue agent in the FBI would be complicit with such an underworld organization, sometimes it's wisest to address such possibilities before they happen. Oh, and one more thing, Ron. While duplicating evidence can be a good thing to ensure it isn't later tampered with, stolen or destroyed...on the other hand, we don't want too many copies made, because then you could lose leverage on future value."

Turning off the Dallas-Fort Worth Turnpike, Worth pulled up to an FBI complex located appropriately enough, at 1 Justice Drive. Walking from the parking lot toward the main building, Worth looked at Winston.

"You nervous?"

"Yeah."

"That's what I like. An honest client."

After walking through a metal detector and several body searches, Winston and Worth were escorted into an anteroom. They didn't wait long.

"Hello, are you Dennis?"

Worth and the FBI head exchanged handshakes.

"Yes, pleased to meet you Mr. Director."

"And you're Mr. Winston?"

"Ron."

"Pleased to meet you both."

The director smiled and motioned them to a meeting room. "I want to apologize to you both for your recent unfortunate incident."

Worth held both hands up. "No problem, Mr. Director. We understand how stressful your jobs are."

"Well, it's very gracious of you to say that. But having worked early in my career with men…and in those days it was all men…who were on detail in Dealey Plaza during the shooting, I can't say how much we appreciate your coming to us first about this evidence."

"Glad to be of assistance, Mr. Director."

"Let's start with what it is you're seeking."

Worth sat up in his chair.

"Certainly, sir. We understand the importance of getting this evidence to the bureau. So aside from assisting you as much as possible, we simply hoped for immunity from any and all charges potentially relating to our possession of the film and bureau assistance for a vigorous defense, if necessary, of the film's ownership by my client."

The Director leaned back in his plush leather chair.

"Anything else?"

"No. That's it."

"That's all?"

"Yes."

The Director smiled.

"We can do that. How soon are you prepared to transfer the evidence to us?"

"So you'll grant my client complete immunity and vigorously defend his claim to ownership of the film, provided we cooperate fully?"

"That's my plan, counselor."

"Once I can review your documents, it sounds like we've got a deal and it could happen very quickly. Possibly this week."

"Great. I'll draft a memo today and have our legal team follow up within the next 72 hours to formalize our agreement."

"Terrific. We'll be waiting."

"One more thing, Mr. Worth."

"Yes."

"Have you seen the film?"

"No, but my client has," Worth said, motioning to Winston.

"Mr. Winston. Do you have any doubt that the film involves the John F. Kennedy assassination?"

"No, sir. It's definitely the president in Dealey Plaza."

"Very good."

On the trip back to Worth's office, Winston shook his head. "Dennis, that was like night and day."

"That's for sure. Now I need to see how fast Mackey can complete his analysis of the film. When I spoke with him yesterday, he said he had a list of things to check on, which is why I was less than specific with the director."

Chapter VI

Castro's Revenge

On a sunny Friday afternoon, Ron Winston was in a mood to kick back for the weekend. Leaving work early, he called his fiance'.

"C'mon, Suze. Let's go dancing. I got some free tickets in the mail to a dance club. It'll be fun."

"I'm sorry, Ron. I can't tonight."

"But you always say you like to dance."

"Since I've had this flu bug, I just don't feel like doing anything. How about next week? Besides, with what you've been going through lately, you could probably use some down time, too."

"Do you still want to do something tomorrow night?"

"Of course. I'm just feeling lagged today and definitely not like dancing."

"Okay. Suit yourself. I might see if the guys at work have a poker game going."

"Love ya, Ron."

"Love you, too, Suze."

Given the stress he'd been under, Winston soon realized it'd be nice to blow off some steam. His anxiety was nothing a good night out couldn't fix. Besides, he hadn't used his dance lessons in several months. Winston pulled a sports jacket from the closet and walked to his waiting Saab. Twenty minutes later, he was a few blocks from Caliente', a trendy downtown dance club in old Dallas.

After a short walk from his car in the dry night air, Winston passed through the entrance to surrender the complimentary 'no cover charge' ticket he'd received. Descending into a party-like atmosphere, at the center of a dimly-lit floor danced half a dozen couples to a lively five piece Mariachi band. Several stood at tiny tables barely large enough to hold their drinks. Winston advanced to the bar.

"What'll you have?"

"Draft beer if you've got it."

"Sure—Dos Equis. Ten bucks."

Winston dug deep into his pocket and placed two wadded fivers on the bar. Sipping the frosty pint, he sensed a tap on his shoulder, followed by a sultry voice with a heavy Spanish accent.

"Do you come here often? I think we've not met."

Winston swiveled on his barstool. The stunning brunette's face seemed vaguely familiar.

"It's my first time here."

"What you think?"

"I don't know yet—it's early. Want a seat?"

"Thank you."

As she sat down, her crossed legs revealed a slit on the side of her dress, along with a bit of thigh. Brushing a stray lock of wavy hair out of her eyes, she smiled intensely.

"Do you dance?"

"Not much, but I've had lessons."

The bartender reappeared. "What'll it be, Maria?"

"Cerveza."

"Coming up."

As Winston strained to hear past the loud music, he realized he'd never seen such bright red lipstick. "I take it you're a regular here?"

Maria ignored Winston's question. Her demeanor suddenly turned serious.

"Can I ask something to you?"

"Sure."

"Why come here, if not to dance?"

Winston smirked before pouring on his salesman charm.

"Don't tell me dancing's a requirement to have a beer. Maybe I'm just shy and hoping to meet someone like you."

She smiled, revealing blindingly white teeth.

"You seem not shy to me."

"Then I guess we both know the answer."

"Really," she continued. "Do you dance?"

"Even after some classes, I'm still unsure out there," Winston said, nodding toward the dance floor. "Maybe I should learn more by watching others first."

Maria laughed and threw her head back, accentuating a plunging neckline.

"You must *do*, not only watch."

Standing abruptly in her red stiletto heels, Maria looked directly into Ron's eyes. Extending a well manicured hand, she mouthed sensuously: "Here…I show you." As Maria pulled him toward the dance floor, Winston grimaced while his thoughts raced. *Great. Now I get to look like an idiot in front of people who know what they're doing.*

The click-clack of Maria's shoes were Winston's countdown to humiliation. She sensed his embarrassment.

"Consider this a free lesson, then." Winston understood her point. As a new song began, he considered taking advantage of the opportunity to learn from an apparent expert.

"Ah, Rhumba...I KNOW this dance," Winston said.

Arching her body gracefully, Maria's right hand fluttered between their faces. Winston grasped it. Maria nodded in agreement. As they moved in unison, he noticed her perfume smelled like fresh lilac.

"Rhumba is a sensual dance," Maria whispered. "It is not about speed. Like all dance, it is about, how you say...enjoying the moment."

Winston's feet began moving in the diamond pattern of international Rhumba, the only style he knew. As they held each other, he spoke softly: "My instructor told me international is the one to learn. That way I can dance with women from different countries."

"True," Maria smiled. "The American version is fun, but not so well-known outside of the USA. You're good for a beginner. How long you take lessons?"

"Four months. They weren't cheap, either. I'm glad you think I got my money's worth."

The music continued as their bodies intertwined in rhythm.

"Do you Tango or Paso Doble?" Maria wondered aloud.

"Whoa. One dance at a time. I barely know Rhumba."

"That is no problem. I can always use a new dance partner. I will teach you."

As the music ended, the two returned to their barstools. Winston sensed Maria was more than casually interested. Maybe too interested. *I've already got a fiance'*, Winston reminded himself. *Besides, when it comes to women, two is one too many.*

Cha-Cha music began and Winston turned to Maria. "So, are you always looking for new dance partners?"

"You seem like a nice person. Why not?"

As they both laughed, Winston felt his mouth work in slow motion. Straining to keep his eyes open, he tried to speak. "I'm getting tirrrr......"

Seconds later, he was out cold. A thirty-ish man several seats down the bar ran over.

"Is he OK? I know CPR."

Maria smiled.

"No, he is fine—Just too much cerveza. We will give him a ride home."

Maria waved her hand at the bartender. "Ricardo."

Winston was hoisted up and over the husky man's shoulders. Feet dragging, Winston was carried through the kitchen door and into a waiting van.

"Rapido, rapido," the bartender yelled, slamming the door. Dusting his hands off, he turned to Maria. "Viva Fidel." Maria smiled. "Viva Fidel."

Hours later, Winston began to stir. He shivered as his eyes opened to the cold darkness. *My head,* Winston thought. Picking himself up, the vibrations of a low-pitched engine rumbled gutturally in the background. Inhaling deeply, Winston's nostrils stung from the odorous mixture of brine and diesel fuel. His body pitched every few seconds to the motion of waves.

"Must be a ship of some kind and I'm in the hold." As he looked around in an attempt get his bearings, Winston recalled his dance partner from what seemed like a day before. Recounting his last drink, he heard faint voices directly above him. Winston stood up quietly.

"Sounds like the welcoming committee on a slow boat to nowhere," he mused. "When will this stop?" Feeling despair, Winston knelt and closed his eyes as hard metal rhythmically pushed against his kneecaps. "Lord, I can't change my past. And my present isn't looking so good, either. But my future hasn't been written yet. Please help me out of here. Amen."

In the blackness, Winston felt around, grasped what seemed like a long, cold pipe along one wall and hoisted himself up. Head throbbing harder, Winston gripped tightly and continued his ascent. His skull bumped metal. Feeling a handle, he turned it, pushed hard and a hatch door flung open. Eyes adjusting to the light, he heard only "Gringo!"

"Terrific," Winston groaned. Looking around the trawler-like boat deck, he quickly realized there were two choices. Either duke it out with at least one burly type, or take a swim. He was overboard and in the cold water in seconds. Holding his breath for as long as possible, Winston came up for air about twenty yards from the ship. Water erupted all around him.

Pitack. Phew. Phew.

"Great…just great. These dudes are trigger happy."

Winston dove deep and swam away from the ship. Breaking surface briefly for air, he descended again, swimming the underwater breaststroke toward a pale blinking buoy he'd noticed several hundred feet away. By the time he re-emerged, the ship was circling farther out. Dunking once more, Winston worked underwater toward the bobbing buoy. Finally touching it, he swam underneath. Winston reached through the water with one hand to feel inside the buoy. "Hollow. Alright."

Submerging again, he rose, with his head now inside the large cone of floating metal. A tinny echo rang in his ears. Moments later, he heard the craft's engines grow louder, then fade as it circled ever-wider. Within minutes, the hostile ship seemed gone. Uncertain if the engines were silenced to wait him out, Winston gulped a big breath of air and emerged briefly to scan the area. "Nothing," he convinced himself. Peering with his fast-numbing grasp on the buoy, his adrenaline subsided.

"Man, it's cold—I better get moving. Waiting won't make this any easier." Winston began slow, steady crawl strokes toward what he guessed might be land. Using a distant flashing buoy as his reference point, Winston hoped to head straight toward it and the nighttime aura that shone above. Twenty minutes later, the buoy he left seemed very distant. Focusing intently on the soft lightscape before him, Winston switched to a more relaxed breast-stroke. He traveled slower, but at least his head could remain above water. Thirty minutes later, a tired Winston saw another buoy. Soon another, spaced much closer this time. Then another.

"Those have to be channel markers," Winston breathed. "I must be near land."

Invigorated with hope and new-found energy, Winston switched back to the crawl stroke and soon detected lights several hundred yards from the mouth of what appeared to be a main waterway...and shore. Fifteen minutes later, waves crashed over him as he crawled onto sand and rolled over, shivering and exhausted.

"Now what," he wondered minutes later, too tired to think much beyond getting warm. The distant sound of an approaching car gave Winston incentive to get off the beach and find cover fast. Scurrying to a large log, he began to dig using a bucket-sized shell to afford himself maximum invisibility.

Before long, Winston was mostly covered in sand. He placed a now-soggy handkerchief over his face to breathe. Piling on more sand, Winston made sure to keep his ears uncovered to ensure he could still hear. A vehicle drove nearby then the engine stopped. *I wonder if they saw me,* Winston thought, now taking shallow breaths.

Car doors slammed. Moments later came two voices. Both spoke English but it was neither one's native tongue. The husky male voice was tinged with a Russian accent. Another was that of a staccato-speaking woman with a Spanish accent.

"They said this way," groused the man.

"He could be anywhere," she said.

The man waited before responding: "That is, if he's still alive." Then came a laugh, followed by an emphysemic hack.

"So we wait for someone who is probably dead, then?"

"Let me call our former CIA friend."

A chill ran down Winston's spine as he thought about what he'd just heard. *Former CIA friend?*

Moments later, the talking resumed. "Helmut? Raoul. There is no one here." After a long pause, the man's voice continued. "Then bring the thermal imaging helicopter. We must leave now."

Car doors slammed as the car sped off. Still lying under the sand, two things became clear to Winston. One was that he better hightail it out fast, or risk discovery by high tech gadgetry. And second, a mole deep inside the CIA wanted him captured...or dead. Yet Winston still didn't have a clue where in the world he was.

With the car's engine now out of audible range, Winston slowly arose, pulling the clammy handkerchief off his face. Peeking over the driftwood, he had to find a phone. But Winston could barely keep his eyes open. First came sleep. Across the road he noticed what looked like an abandoned construction site. Off to one side were several large cement culverts, perfect for hiding. Winston crawled inside. Realizing thermal imaging might not easily penetrate cement, he relaxed and was soon dozing.

Winston woke to a growling stomach and realized he had no idea where he'd landed. Overwhelmed by hunger and fear, he felt despair. What scared him most was that he simply had no idea where he was. Winston began to pray and eventually felt renewed.

Given the apparently sparse local population, he headed out to survey the area and located an old boarded-up gas station. Next to it was a phone booth. He cautiously picked up the phone and heard a dial tone. "That answers my prayers…now hopefully someone answers my call." Punching numbers, Winston heard a ring, then an operator's voice in Spanish.

"Do you speak English?"

"Uno momento." After a few moments, Winston heard a series of clicks, a loud hum, then a voice.

"May I help you?"

"Yes, I'm trying to make a collect call to the United States."

"I'll connect you—What is the number?"

I don't happen to have it with me, but I'm calling for Dennis Worth, an attorney in the Dallas, Texas metroplex.

In minutes, the line buzzed through a crackling phone connection.

"Law office of Dennis Worth."

The operator broke in. "Yes, I have a collect call for Dennis Worth."

"Who is calling?"

"My name is Ron Winston. Dennis, please."

"I'm sorry. He's in a meeting."

"Sir? This is the operator. Do you wish to call back later?"

"No. Please tell the other party that Ron Winston is on the line and it's important."

Worth's receptionist responded with "Please hold and I'll see if he can be reached."

Winston breathed deeply and waited. Then sounded a pronounced 'click.'

"Ron—Where are you?"

"Dennis, I'm not sure. But I jumped off a ship and am glad just to be alive."

"Let me put you on hold while I see if we can have the call traced, okay?"

"By whom?"

"So we don't put all our eggs in one basket, I've established a relationship not only with the FBI, but also the CIA…just in case. If you're in country, I'd recommend we contact the FBI to find you. But if you think you might be outside US borders, the CIA is a better bet. They have a broader reach."

"Dennis, I have no idea where I am."

"Have you heard only English spoken?"

"Let's just say there have been plenty of different languages."

"Sounds international to me."

"Fine. Just do something, please."

Several minutes later, a terse voice joined on the line, making it a three-way phone call. "Case officer Frey, here. Is this Mr. Winston?"

"Yes."

"We're now locating your whereabouts via phone trace."

Half-standing in a crouch as low as the phone cord would allow, Winston's head swiveled frantically as he continued peering outside the phone booth. "Mr. Frey, I think it's some of *your* guys who are trying to kill me."

"Pardon?"

"You're a case officer?"

"That's right."

"With the CIA?"

"Correct."

"Mr. Frey, someone with CIA affiliations already *knows* where I am, and he's trying to either capture or kill me."

There was a pause. "Where did you receive this information?"

Worth interjected in an uneven voice. "Ron. We're taking a chance here. But Mr. Frey has assured me he has the capacity to help find you so we can get you back here safely. But it's your call. If you feel compromised, hang up now."

"Dennis…"

Frey resumed speaking. "Mr. Winston—since I'm not there, I can't say with 100% accuracy what's going on. But if what you just said is true, either you're dealing with people who SAID they have CIA ties, or a rogue agent acting alone. In either case, I can only attempt to provide you with safe passage out of there if you stay on the line and allow the trace to complete."

"How will you pick me up?"

"We have a chopper on standby right now."

"Alright. I'll tell you what. I've got a red handkerchief in my back pocket. Unless I get shot trying, when you tell me to hang up I'm going to tie it to a bar on top of the phone booth and stay within sight. If I see your chopper and if it looks legit, I'm there. Otherwise, if any more goons try tracking my carcass, they're going to have a hard time finding me. And if I get my hands on them, they just may end up as carcasses, themselves."

Frey broke back in: "Mr. Winston, we're narrowing down your location. One moment."

Winston's heart pounded. "Dennis—If anything happens to me, you have to believe what I'm saying. I overheard several people with accents. One guy mentioned they had a CIA insider feeding them intel on me."

Worth responded: "Ron, I understand your concern. But there's a certain degree of trust necessary to…"

"Got it," Frey confirmed then hung up in the background on his other phone call, before re-joining Ron and Dennis. "Okay, here's the deal. Ron, we've just determined you're presently near the tip of what's called the Sabana-Camaguey Archipelago. From the best we can tell, you've likely traveled from a nearby port, perhaps the friendly Bahamas, right into communist waters. We've scrambled a chopper and it's now headed your way. But be prepared for a little excitement. Though we'll be 'in and out' of country *fast* to pick you up, the government of Cuba doesn't take too kindly to our exercises in the area. As a result, the American philosophy in this kind of situation is that it's better to ask forgiveness than permission. ETA is 29 minutes."

Winston exhaled deeply. "There's some brush within 100 feet of the phone booth and a sand parking lot next to both. You might be able to land your chopper there. I'll be waiting."

Frey spoke in a slow, deliberate tone.

"Mr. Winston?"

"Yes."

"We may only get one chance to do this, so let me say three things to prepare you, real quick.

"Go for it."

"Number one, once the chopper has landed...and not before..."

"Yes?"

"Run fast, but stay very low."

"Got it."

"Number two, so our chopper personnel know who's getting on board, the code will be the last four digits of your social security number, which we have here."

"Okay."

"You don't give him the right code, you're offa there."

"Alright…So, what's number three?"

"A government records search indicates you're a concealed carry permit holder.

"Right…I'm a real estate agent and sometimes work in bad neighborhoods."

"That's fine. Number three is that once you're on board, you may be provided with a weapon in the event there is return enemy fire.

Winston responded unenthusiastically. "Enemy fire. Great. What other option do I have now, anyway?" he uttered.

"We're going in fast, light and low under the radar, so the pilot will need both hands and as few distractions as possible to make a fast insertion and extraction. You comfortable with a 9mm semi-automatic?

"I own one myself."

"Perfect. Then that's it…Roger and out. Your pickup is now twenty six minutes away. Godspeed."

"Bye," Winston responded as he exited the phone booth, lowered himself and crawled quickly to nearby brush surrounded by an occasional palm tree, hoping no one saw him. From his vantage point, he had a view of the parking lot and beach, both less than a football field away. The low hum was at first barely audible. In a minute or so, the helicopter sounded like a fully loaded washing machine on high spin cycle.

Winston peered from his hunkered-down position and watched as the chopper approached so low on the horizon its landing apparatus skimmed a few waves. But something was wrong. As the aircraft approached, it began to drift, remaining parallel to the beach. Winston hadn't yet been spotted, nor had the pilot seen his handkerchief on the phone booth. Before the craft could move too far, Ron sucked in a big breath of air and darted from the brush, waving his hands.

"Over here. Over here."

Ka-phew.

Sand exploded near Winston's feet, stinging his legs. Now at a full-out sprint, he ran directly at the approaching copter, arms flailing like a madman. "Over here! Over here!"

He next felt something burn in his shoulder. All of a sudden, Winston's left arm wouldn't move. "Ohhhhhh...no."

What happened next seemed to happen in slow motion. The helicopter lowered and landed within feet of Winston. He crawled up, throwing himself on the craft's floor.

"What's the code," barked a camouflaged form inside, cradling what looked like a gatling gun.

"4-1-3-3."

The soldier spoke into a headset attached to his helmet. "Roger that...extract...extract!" With a loud

"Whoosh," the copter accelerated while rising off the ground.

Winston's camo-clad savior announced: "Here's your weapon. I just took out the guy who winged you."

"Thanks," Winston said, out of breath. "How bad's my shoulder?"

"Roll over. Not too bad. You're lucky—that is, if you're right handed."

"Am I bleeding?"

"Not much. Thankfully, these Cubans don't have much spare ammo for practice. Looks like it went clean through, too and missed any major blood vessels. We'll have a doc check you out on landing. In this rig at our present speed, that should be about 25 minutes, max."

As the chopper prepared to touch down, a weary Winston began to assess his situation. *I need to see Dennis*, he thought. *I'm done with this. I want my life back.* Then everything went black. Waking up later in a hospital bed, Winston opened his eyes to see none other than Dennis Worth sitting by his bedside.

"Ron—how're you doing?"

"Dennis. I'm tired of being a target."

Chapter VII

Wayne's World

It usually took Wayne Schaefer a four hour drive to reach the underground rural Oklahoma airstrip CIA operatives called 'The Foxhole.' Schaefer knew the way well, having made many a 'dead drop' nearby and conducted interrogations in nondescript offices there. Given the decent weather and light traffic, tonight Schaefer was certain he could make it in record time.

As he crossed the Texas—Oklahoma border under a near-full moon, the region's flat, desolate countryside unfolded before him. Schaefer began to imagine the questions he would be asked. Schaefer approached the secured perimeter near his rendezvous and pulled out his ID. Looking at his watch, he chuckled. "1:44 AM. Looks like I made pretty good time." Slowing his SUV at the station manned by a two well-armed guards, he was waved through.

"Go on in. Your ride's waiting for you, sir."

Schaefer nodded, drove ahead and noticed the whine of jet engines inside a nearby football stadium-like structure. He parked on the other end of the complex, then grabbed his overnight bag. Schaefer slammed his car door and ran, head low, toward the waiting aircraft. He strained to hear the pilot while lumbering aboard.

"Going to Maryland?"

"That's me," Schaefer replied.

"I'm Captain Heywood. We'll be flying at a steady clip and should arrive at our destination in a little more than two hours. Take a nap if you'd like. There's a cot in back."

Schaefer grinned.

"Thanks, Captain. No problem."

The pilot nodded, straining to speak over engine noise.

"There's also a stuffed fridge and full bar. But let me know if you need anything else. You're apparently pretty important cargo."

Schaefer feigned surprise. "Really? How's that?"

"We've got an escort," he yelled pointing a thumb toward the window. Schaefer glanced outside the stadium-like complex and saw two fighter jets within a hundred yards as they began to scramble.

"What the…" Schaefer said.

"Don't worry. They're here to make sure I take good care of you."

The moment Schaefer sat on the lone cot in back of the aircraft, he realized how tired he was. "I could use some sleep. Maybe the turbulence will be minimal and I can bag some z's."

"Here," the pilot said, tossing Schaefer a set of earplugs. "These help, too."

"Thanks."

After an uneventful, if somewhat bumpy flight, a semi-rested Wayne Schaefer rolled off his cot to the sound of slowing jet engines. He walked toward the now-open door. Shaking the pilot's hand, they were greeted with the rising sun.

"Thanks, Captain. I appreciate your helping me get a little shut-eye."

"We do the best we can...sometimes the weather makes it a little difficult. Good luck to you on whatever mission you have here."

Stepping down from the aircraft, Schaefer noticed they still had company. "Those fighters follow us here?"

"The whole way. I felt a little nervous, because while refueling before we left, I noticed their wing guns weren't loaded with the usual 'dummy' rounds. But hey, I just do the hauling. Besides, I keep my security clearance by not asking questions."

Plenty of 'higher-ups' in military intelligence passed through this little-known hot spot of international intrigue. Given its low profile compared to CIA locations like Langley, Virginia, key spy functions were more covertly performed here. Word was even the Russians and Chinese didn't yet know the place existed. Walking off the tarmac, Schaefer headed directly for the unmapped airstrip's canteen.

Government-run and always open, Schaefer learned to skip eating on inbound trips to make maximum room for legendary meals here. Given ample classified budgets, government patrons could requisition home-cooked food at any hour, all prepared by chefs recruited from some of the world's finest restaurants. Along with legendary dry-aged meats, the Crème brûlée was to die for. Schaefer was famished and got right to work on breakfast. After an order of rib eye hash with sunny side up farm fresh eggs, fried Idaho potatoes and several cups of fresh coffee, Schaefer felt alive again.

"Now to clean up," he told himself. Down an adjacent terminal, he entered a steamy locker room and tossed his overnight bag on a wall hook inside a specially encrypted locker keyed to his fingerprint. Ten minutes later, he grabbed a towel and dried himself off. "Wow. That felt good." Adjusting his necktie, he spoke to the mirror: "Next up, Ol' Bailey."

Schaefer walked aboveground for a few minutes, then descended through a series of maze-like staircases. Traversing the well-lit underground pathway, he passed through a series of tunnel security check-points—each requiring a retina scan—before proceeding to the last of the large campus-like structures. Schaefer trod up a massive stairwell to familiar carpeted hallways. He nodded 'Hello' to one security guard in the main hall and entered the waiting room of his old case officer. Softly closing the door behind him, he took a seat. A pleasant middle-aged female clerk behind a glass window immediately took notice.

"May I help you?"

"Oh, no worries. I'm Wayne Schaefer. Ol' Bailey is expecting me."

"Ol' Bailey?"

"Sorry," Schaefer intoned. "Mr. Bailey."

Looking up at his watch, Schaefer thought calmly. *9:00 AM sharp. Should be any second now.* Within moments, Schaefer heard a familiar voice greet someone in the hallway.

"Have a nice morning."

"You, too, Louis."

Schaefer chuckled silently. "Still the same old Bailey...you can set your watch to him." CIA supervisor Louis Bailey hurriedly opened the door and entered the waiting room. A small balding, pinstripe-suited man with a round paunch, he carried a large black briefcase. Schaefer's old boss was hardly leading man material. Instead, he resembled a doughy, middle-aged appliance repairman. Noticing Schaefer, Bailey stopped, puzzled.

"Wayne—you been waiting long?

"Naw. Just got here."

"Glad to see you," Bailey replied in an unconvincing tone. "Looks like you're my first appointment this morning. What brings you all the way back here today?"

"I thought *you* were going to tell *me*," Schaefer said sarcastically.

Embarrassed, Bailey hurriedly ushered Schaefer inside his office. Closing the door, he motioned to Schaefer.

"Have a seat, Wayne."

"Don't mind if I do."

Walking across the room to his large oak desk, Bailey sat behind it, swiveled to face Wayne Schaefer and folded his hands.

"So really, what are we here to discuss?"

Schaefer sneered.

"I dunno, boss. You're the one who said it was time to retire the 'old guard.'"

"Wayne, you know that was on orders from above."

Schaefer pulled a small square box from his coat and laid it on the desk between them.

"Then this might help you re-think the elimination strategy you bought into when so many of us were told to 're-orient' for different careers."

Bailey glanced briefly at the box in front of him.

"Wayne, whatever this is about, you know I don't make the rules. Everything back then was way beyond my…"

Schaefer looked heavenward and opened his palms, looking martyr-like.

"You could have at least stood up for me, Bailey…like I repeatedly did for you. As I recall, in the early days, my testimony once helped you to get just a reprimand…instead of canned."

"Wayne, we agreed to never discuss that again."

Schaefer exhaled and looked out through the adjacent window.

"So we did."

Bailey scooted his chair close toward the desk and laid his eyeglasses to one side.

"So what is this about?"

"Seriously, Bailey. They didn't brief you yet?"

"Yesterday I heard *you'd* be briefing *me*, but wasn't told what it was about…or that you'd be here in person to do it."

Schaefer smiled.

"Then pick the biggest unsolved mystery you can think of."

"Hoffa."

"Bigger."

"Amelia Earhart."

"Bigger."

"Bigger?"

"*Waaay* bigger."

"Foreign or domestic?"

"Both."

"JFK," Bailey said without missing a beat.

"Bingo."

Bailey pointed at the package on his desk. "Wayne, what is this, really?"

"Bailey, we've had our differences. Yet unlike you, I still feel I owe you a degree of loyalty, given the work we've done together in the past. As my supervisor, I want you in on this."

Fighting a smirk, Schaefer next laid it on with a trowel: "Besides, it doesn't hurt that you're the best in the business."

Bailey turned red. "You're very kind, Wayne and I've always appreciated your loyalty."

He pointed at the small packet on his desk.

"Wayne—It's not a bomb, is it?"

Schaefer chuckled. "Yeah, right...like I'm going to get within a mile of here with something like that." Schaefer reached into his pants pocket and pulled out a stick of gum. Preparing to reel in his well-hooked quarry, Schaefer began to chew slowly for effect.

"Now I'm not certain, Bailey. But what's on your desk right now *could* provide some additional information on what went down in Dealey Plaza on November 22, 1963. Got it from one of my Dallas area contacts, as a matter of fact."

Rising from his chair, Bailey's arms widened out across the desk to grasp each end, eyes fixed intently on the package. He alternately shifted his eyes to Schaefer, then the package.

"Give me the back story to what you've got, so we can walk through this together."

Schaefer paused with relish. "Well, a kid my son grew up with happens to work in a camera shop. It may be small-town irony, but his dad's a long-retired CIA operative—Hollister—and a close friend of mine from my time overseas."

Bailey looked puzzled.

"Hollister. Gordon Hollister?"

"That's him."

"I knew Gordon Hollister, Wayne, but that would have been a long while ago. Kenya, I think. Anyway, go on."

"So, we get to talking at a wedding a while back and you know me...always on the lookout for new recruits. Anyway, the kid seemed disinterested in agency work. But a few weeks after I pushed him hard to consider a CIA career, he shows up at my doorstep and wants to talk. Then he tells me about a 'weird' film he developed and gives me a copy. Come to find out that a never-seen film of the JFK assassination may have been up in a Texas attic for all these decades."

Bailey's jaw practically hit his protruding paunch.

"What does it show, Wayne?"

Schaefer decided to let out a little more line to play with his old boss. "You even interested?"

"Are you kidding? Of course!"

"Actually, it's too early to tell," Schaefer said nonchalantly.

"Have forensics been done yet?"

"It hasn't been analyzed. You know better than me these days, but from what I understand, the lab can work wonders with all their computer capabilities. I know it's Kennedy in Dealey Plaza and the film quality is pretty good."

Bailey looked out the window and frowned. "Wayne, you know what this means."

"That we'll finally catch those responsible for the death of the president and vindicate the CIA?"

"No. We need to disclose this ASAP, otherwise heads will roll. And I don't know about you, but I want to retain my pension."

Schaefer shook his head. "Bailey. Even after all these years, you never cease to amaze me. I bring you evidence that could blow the lid completely off unknown details of a presidential assassination, and you're concerned about intra-agency protocol? So *that's* why we're losing on so many fronts."

"But Wayne, you know what happens when we don't follow procedure."

"Procedure? Protocol? Pensions? Are you serious? You're talking to the wrong guy, Bailey. Besides—don't you remember? I lost my chance for a pension years ago."

Bailey averted Schaefer's glare. "The Bailey I *used* to know wasn't afraid of 'mixing things up' when it was the right thing to do. Have you become *completely* co-opted by the 'suits' upstairs?"

Bailey swiveled in his executive chair and looked out the window. Still avoiding Schaefer's gaze, he slowly clicked a ballpoint pen and listened.

"Any way you slice it, Bailey, letting this kind of evidence slip through our fingers while we wait for CIA forensics to get a firm grasp of what we're dealing with is a *very* bad move. Deep down, I think even you know that. Once again, if we don't run ahead of this and fast, it'll only increase our risk of getting the short end of the stick...again...in any dealings with the FBI. You better consider getting our technical people on this right away, before word gets out in the entire intel community."

Schaefer was on a roll and continued. "You know how it works, Bailey. Once the FBI finds out, they'll not just take credit for finding this film. A few of those conniving, back-stabbing, glory hogs will say it further proves the CIA was in on a coup. If things aren't done differently when it comes to an investigation this old, our own CIA bureaucrats will only screw it up, just like before. Why would you honestly think they'd do any different?"

"So when do you suggest we inform upper management, Wayne?"

"Once we know what we've got and we're sure it's safe to bring out. While our labs work the technical side, we also need someone deep undercover to ferret out the background on this stuff—like who *is* this guy that surfaced with the film? Was it planted? Is he a foreign national?"

"Let me guess who you propose should go deep undercover?"

"That's right, Bailey. *Moi.*"

Schaefer's old boss pointed to the package on the table between them. "Wayne, why go deep undercover? We've *got* the evidence."

"That's just it. Before ANYTHING comes out on the film's findings, we have to be ready to pounce anywhere and anyhow. For all we know and as much as I hate to admit it, this film might even implicate OUR people. So this has to be pursued differently and cover has to be *extra* deep. Besides, you know how porous decent intel is in Washington."

Schaefer tapped his finger on the desk between them. "Bailey, mark my words. Once this gets into the hands of the 'suits,' some wannabe insider trying for an 'in' to 'A' list Christmas parties will phone the media in a matter of hours...that is, if he isn't already on their payroll."

"Wayne, you know how the game is played to keep this kind of thing quiet. In addition to summary dismissal, any deviation from standard operating procedure is inviting a subpoena, complete with sealed records, making our legal defense impractical. Plus, there's possible jail time in store once it's determined we sat on intelligence this potentially explosive. We both know it's simply not enough to only inform forensics. Agency higher-ups have a need to know. They hate to be blindsided by this kind of stuff."

Schaefer's face lit up as he slapped Bailey's desk. "Bailey, I've got an idea."

"I was afraid of that."

"No, really. How about giving me a few days under deep cover with the tools I need?"

"Wayne, what are you talking about?"

"My old crew," Schaefer said quietly.

"You've *got* to be kidding," Bailey spat out. "That bunch of anti-social misfits?"

"Look, we've gone over this before. They were the best in the business...they're just not cookie-cutter types."

"That's for sure. That group you ran with are more like wad-cutter types. Talk about a bunch of loose cannons. Especially Rico. You're really kidding, right?"

"No, I'm not kidding at all. Now remember— I've done some great work, even if it wasn't always by the book. And before you get tied up in knots about Rico, remember—he earned the Bronze Star and a Purple Heart. As his Skipper, I can say he's always been loyal and focused on the mission at hand. Besides, Bailey...if it weren't for me, you wouldn't have a clue about what's going down right now. I came to you first with this."

Bailey shook his head. "Wayne, you know I don't have the authority to withhold reporting this, so please don't even ask."

"I'm not asking you to withhold anything...at least for long. Just give me what I need: My crew and a few days. I'll get to the bottom of this. And think of it, Bailey. If any pantywaist 'higher-ups' ride you, you can simply tell them the intel wasn't quashed at all...merely postponed, while we review our most prudent options. Besides, this is even better than 'under the radar.' If we do it my way, we'll have it off the screen entirely. Plus, since I still have a few of my old clearances, that should prevent them from coming down on you. It's perfect— plausible deniability. You can shift the blame directly onto me."

Bailey managed a smile, looking like he actually wanted to buy it. "What's *really* behind this, Wayne? Still trying to prove yourself?"

Schaefer stood and walked to the window. "I figured you'd say that, Bailey. Think whatever you want, but you know I've paid my dues. And when it comes to something like this, don't be mad at me—neither of us blew the original Kennedy investigation. But since I'm currently being 'phased out' of the agency's plans, at least give me a chance to prove my worth with something that matters for a change."

"Wayne, you know this is going to need at the very least, committee authorization."

Schaefer turned from the window and sneered at Bailey. "Committee authorization? We're dealing with something as monumental as the JFK assassination and YOU'RE worried about committee authorization from a bunch of career pencil-pushers? These are the same kind of office types that Monday morning quarterback every tough field decision people like me make. Besides, it's my literal butt on the line, while theirs are planted firmly in soft leather chairs. Committee authorization," Schaefer said in long syllables as his boss looked at the floor. "Bailey, do you realize how crazy that sounds to those of us who live in the real world?"

Louis Bailey swiveled in his chair, crossing his legs. "Wayne, I understand your frustration. And to be honest, I halfway agree with you. Here's what I *can* do. And in the end, you'll have access to far more resources than I'd normally have the capacity to underwrite. I'll call a special meeting of our covert ops group directors. Minutes of our meeting would only be used to record those in attendance—no other notes of any kind. That way, we're working *within* the system. It'll be safer that way in case things don't work out and we get second-guessed. And you still won't have to worry about cover being blown, or media exposure, since everyone in the group has 'top secret' clearance. Trust me. Those people simply don't talk."

Wayne Schaefer was non-plussed.

"Let me get this straight, Bailey. You're going to pitch my idea for deep cover to a bunch of bureaucrats who've developed covering their fannies into an art form?"

Bailey shifted nervously in his chair as Schaefer continued. "Not only that. These are the same people, 'within the system' as you say, who could easily throw a monkey wrench to prevent their own inertia from being noticed...or worse."

Bailey looked genuinely baffled. "Worse? Wayne, just what are you getting at?"

"Think about it, Bailey. If the JFK assassination was indeed an 'inside job' as some outside the agency postulate...and committed on behalf of the so-called 'military-industrial complex,' where does that finger point? Remember, fish rots from the head first."

Schaefer saw he had Bailey's rapt attention and continued. "You know I'm a CIA loyalist. I've laid my life on the line for this agency more than once. But we need a clean look at the *whole* mess and it has to be above-board this time. We have to go where the trail leads. No exceptions. Otherwise, we'll all be accused of a whitewash and good luck ever getting another shot at doing the right thing again if *that* happens. What we need now is an intra-agency audit. And I'm the auditor."

Bailey threw his hands up in a feigned act of surrender. "My idea is best, Wayne. Otherwise, under standard procedure I'll have to submit this for committee review and neither of us wants to wait for it to wend its way up the chain of command. Besides, doing that could take a month and involve even more of the pencil-pushers you dislike. To make matters worse, standard committee review aides hold only 'secret' clearance...at best. On the other hand, the covert ops meeting convenes at least weekly."

"Okay, Bailey. We have our disagreements. But let's agree on one thing. No matter what the film reveals, no one will remember who gets to it second. The CIA needs to go where it leads...and first." For the first time that morning, Bailey looked genuinely proud. "Agreed!"

Schaefer sensed Bailey softening and went in for the kill. "Then just give me until that meeting. I only need a little time to investigate the situation and a few bucks to get it done."

"Wayne, that's barely three days away...and we haven't budgeted for it."

"Look—we *both* know you have the discretion to dip into agency contingency funds for urgent covert projects. That's what this is and here's what I need."

Schaefer pulled a sheet of paper from his coat pocket and placed it on the desk between them. Bailey put on his bifocals and began to read aloud:

One: Three dark-colored late-model vehicles, each with tinted glass and unlimited fuel allowance.

Two: Six level-three code-encrypted transmitter/receivers, each equipped with wireless earpiece microphones.

Three: Two dozen 9mm Heckler & Koch semi-automatic handguns—each equipped with six 13-round magazines. Three Finnish .338 Lapua Magnum sniper rifles.

Four: Fresh ID and $25,000 credit card authorization for each designated team member.

Five: Pneumatic earth punch currently sequestered with the Army Corps of Engineers.

Six: Priority access to CIA flight transportation.

Bailey took off his bifocals and looked over at Schaefer. "Earth punch? Never heard of it." Flicking the paper with his index finger, Bailey lowered his voice. "And that's just the first page. Wayne…what is this really all about?"

"It's what you might call a 'modified requisition,' Bailey. Some of it's strictly for contingency planning, in case we get caught and have to bribe our way out. I've learned it's far less costly that way, rather than trying to do it on the cheap and then paying even more in ransom. Plus, if you're ever investigated, suppose they look for any kind of government requisition form. This way you can say you don't have one. And while it lets you know what I need, you'll be in the clear, since you don't have to officially sign or approve anything. It's just between you and me. In fact, before I leave feel free to ignite it with one of those good Cuban cigars I gave you. Given your discretionary budget for urgent covert operations, it's perfect."

Schaefer decided to push his luck. "So, Boss—deal?"

Bailey reexamined the list in his pudgy hands. "Wayne, are you starting a war?"

"No, Bailey. I'm finishing one."

Schaefer's boss looked out the window. "Blazes, Wayne...you're lucky."

Schaefer smiled, sensing his old boss relax. "Lucky? Why's that?"

"Because we *both* know I still owe you one. That...and you can be *very* persistent."

Schaefer smiled as Bailey chewed on one end of his eyeglasses. Suddenly, Bailey spun around and placed both hands flat on his desk.

"Okay, Wayne. I'll give you everything you have on this list. With two conditions."

"Two?"

"Yes, two. One, since this is totally off-budget, please be discrete. No needless 'hot-dogging.' That means keep a collar on your people...especially Rico. At this stage of my career, I don't need anyone coming down on me for bad judgment."

"Okay, fine. I can do discrete. What's number two?"

"Get the job done."

"You got it."

Bailey sighed and rose, his arm extending toward Schaefer. "Deal...but this is doable largely because I'm able to keep it off the record...at least for now, given the purposes of our discussion. Which, by the way, never happened...except possibly under a court-ordered subpoena. So consider this strictly a 'black ops' file."

Schaefer grinned while pushing a business card across Bailey's desk. "You don't have to remind me of plausible deniability, Bailey. I practically invented it. Here's where to send the equipment."

"I'll requisition it this afternoon."

"Thanks, Boss."

Bailey looked at his wristwatch. "See you back here in 71 hours, Wayne. One way or the other."

"You got it."

Wayne Schaefer pointed at the package still on Bailey's desk. "And let me know what forensics finds out about the film."

"Will do, Wayne."

As Schaefer left, Bailey placed the package in his floor safe, closed the round door and twisted the knob. Minutes later, Schaefer was back on an airplane, returning to his original pickup point. For half the trip he napped. During the other half, he laid out a variety of strategic sequences for the upcoming operation and gamed each one in his mind. Minutes after landing, Schaefer pulled out of the parking lot and punched up an old friend on his satellite phone.

"Frank Bishop speaking."

"Bishop. What's the problem with you guys anymore? Do I personally have to visit Langley, Virginia to kick behinds and take names?"

"Sir?"

"It's Wayne. Wayne Schaefer."

"Hey Wayne."

"So Frank—what's up at No Such Agency?"

"We both know the official answer. Not much. How about you, Wayne? What's going on over in your corner of the 'spook' world?"

"Funny you should ask. I have a project I'm getting started on and you're just the person I had in mind."

"I always said someday I'd return the favor I still owe you. I'll never forget how you helped get me airlifted out when those Honduran hit men were about to finish me off."

"Yeah, that was hairy, alright," Schaefer agreed.

"I shudder to think what would've happened if you hadn't given me the 'heads up' in time to get out of there. Wayne, what can I do to finally return the favor?"

"You're encrypted now, right, Frank?"

"Always."

"Okay. Here's what we have. I pulled a file on a guy with the name Ron Winston. He may be a total nobody, but before we undertake anything, I want to be sure."

"Ron Winston. Where's he live and do you have anything else on him?"

Schaefer pulled his car off to the shoulder of the road and rummaged through his file.

"Not a lot else here."

"Can you at least give me a residence address…anything?"

"Oh, sure. He's apparently a real estate agent in the Dallas Metroplex."

"Say no more. That's all I'll need."

"You sure?"

"Oh, yeah. Real estate agents are into self-promotion, big time. They're easy for me to research, like insurance agents, plastic surgeons, dentists and attorneys. Plus, they're licensed with the state. Even with a common name like Ron Winston, if he's around Dallas, I'll have no problem finding him. Piece of cake."

"Great."

"Anything specific you want that I should be looking for?"

"I need his background. I'm guessing there's not much of a rap sheet. But try to find out what kind of a guy he is, any kind of psychographic information. Is he a body-builder, or a bookworm? Weekend warrior or pacifist? That kind of thing, in case we need to take him down."

"I'll get on it." Little more than an hour later, Schaefer's satellite phone buzzed.

"Schaefer here."

"Wayne. It's Frank. I have some news on your guy."

"Speak to me."

"It isn't too good."

"What do you mean?"

"To find much more than his real estate promotional materials, I had to use some heavy-duty programs to lift the lid on this one. That Winston character was apparently under some kind of surveillance."

"Tell me you're joking."

"I wish."

"What else do you know?"

"Looks like he's got a concealed carry permit. And whatever else he may have done, you CIA guys let him get away…right into the arms of the FBI."

Schaefer's stomach sank. "What are you saying, Frank?"

"Wanna hear the audio?"

"Serious? You have that?"

"If you thought our old surveillance software was good, these days I'm as serious as a mortar at close range. The content may make your teeth grind, but the audio quality is good. Here it is. Listen."

Pushing a keyboard button, Bishop connected the stored audio for Schaefer to hear.

"Glad to be of assistance, Mr. Director."

"Let's start with what it is you're seeking, Dennis."

"Certainly, sir. We understand the importance of getting this evidence to the bureau. So aside from assisting you as much as possible, we simply hope for immunity from any and all charges potentially relating to our possession of the film, plus bureau assistance for a vigorous defense, if necessary, of the film's ownership by my client."

"Anything else?"

"No. That's it."

"That's all?"

"Yes."

"We can do that. How soon are you prepared to transfer the evidence to us?"

"So you'll grant my client complete immunity and vigorously defend his claim to ownership of the original film, provided we cooperate fully?"

"That's my plan, counselor."

"Once I can review your documents, it sounds like a deal and it could happen very quickly. Possibly this week. "

"Great. I'll draft a memo today and have our legal team follow up within the next 72 hours to formalize our agreement."

A sound in the background resembled a moving chair.

"Terrific. We'll be waiting."

After a loud 'click,' there was silence.

"Wayne...Wayne...you there?"

"Barely," Schaefer replied.

"How old is that audio?"

"The time stamp shows it was recorded several hours ago."

Schaefer grew upbeat. "Then there's still time."

"What's this about, anyway?"

"I'll give you a hint, Frank. Dealey Plaza."

"Wayne, are you saying the JFK assassination?"

"I am."

"Whoa. Well, if you believe you can run ahead of the FBI once they reach even a verbal agreement, you *are* an optimist. At this point, were this Winston guy to renege, I could see the bureau *really* going after him...on principle, if nothing else."

"No, Frank—listen. Until they reach a signed agreement, everything's still on the table, right?"

Bishop shrugged. "I'm no lawyer, but it sounds like they have an oral understanding of sorts. At least some kind of agreement. Besides, are you seriously thinking about tangling with the bureau on this? I mean, I know sometimes it's a blow to the ego to admit, but at the end of the day, we do all work for the same side."

Schaefer seethed, struggling to remain civil. "Frank, the way the FBI bungled the JFK investigation, then tried shifting their mistakes onto the CIA, sometimes I almost wonder if we do work for the same side. Doesn't that kind of blame game bug you, even as an NSA guy?"

Bishop paused. "Yeah."

Schaefer now had the opening he'd hoped for. "Look...how about I research our options and meet with you later tonight? If we wait beyond that to get started, we'll have lost him for sure. You and I both know that if the FBI co-opts this guy, anything they put out is bound to make both of our organizations look pathetic in the end."

Bishop sighed. "So the NSA and the CIA join forces to battle the wayward FBI. When do you propose we meet?"

"1900 hours."

"Where, Wayne?"

"How about mid-way between Ft. Meade and Langley?"

"Fine. I'm batching it tonight anyway. Let's try College Park. Someone told me about a good Italian place there called Verdi's."

"Never heard of it Frank, but I'll find it. See you there then." Still sitting in his Virginia office an hour later, Frank Bishop picked up his ringing phone.

"Bishop here."

"Hi Frank. It's Michael Collier. 'Upstairs,' as you guys call us. Have a minute?"

"Sure, boss."

"Earlier today I received an automated notice flagging your access of data using one of our hyper-secure networks. Was that breach accidental?"

Bishop took a deep breath. "No."

"Frank, I don't believe you carry the appropriate clearance to access that file. It also appears to be parked inside a 'need to know' database. Care to talk to me about it?"

"He's slipping away," Bishop replied.

"Who?"

"We recently learned of a possible major asset, Mike. I first caught wind of him through CIA agent Wayne Schaefer. I assisted Schaefer using our standard software programs, thinking the old technology would do the job…then things morphed as I saw I'd need a few more software tools. From there, I escalated to a high clearance program. After that I kind of lost track."

"But I never saw a requisition for that, nor would it normally be CIA accessible, save for their highest personnel."

"I realize that. There was a dimension of time-sensitivity here. I've dealt with Schaefer in the past. Not only did he save my bacon with the Honduran assassin fiasco, I understand he does have CIA clearances that would allow him to view some of that material, including parts on the 'need to know.'"

"That helps, especially if he assisted us on the Honduran action. Now I have a better feel about your decision," Collier replied. "But still...looking at what you were delving into, a lot of it is class III, or even higher, 'eyes-only' stuff. What exactly were you working on?"

Bishop stared quietly at the wall. "A bunch of assassination chatter."

"And?"

"We've discerned through intercepted voice and data transmissions that the FBI is now re-opening one of the biggest cases in our lifetime. Think 1963."

"The JFK assassination?"

"Right. Except an individual suspected to have critical evidence on the JFK assassination has slipped right through CIA fingers and into the arms of the bureau."

Collier sighed. "Frank, let's look 'big picture' here. We work with both the CIA and FBI, so other than doing a friend a favor, there's no need to take sides here. But my questions now are how you were able to override our system, then hack into the FBI's encrypted communications?"

"I mainly took advantage of human error to research this particular prospect. First, there were a few 'back doors' I located in our programs. And as far as the FBI, let's just say those guys could use a little brush up on securing their data."

"Do you realize what kind of problems this could cause if it got out?"

"Yes. And about my helping the CIA re-claim an asset targeted by the FBI, I'll admit to feeling conflicted. No one wants war with the bureau. But Schaefer asked me for help and he's a solid, standup guy. I realize here at the NSA, the goal is 'keep a low profile.' Guess I blew it."

Listening intently over the phone, Collier stroked his bearded face with the back of his hand. "Frank, you're right about a low profile being good in our line of work, and for good reason. So remember one thing. When it comes to high profile, the FBI and CIA can both kick our tails in the PR department. Lots of people don't know much about the NSA, but everyone seems to trust the FBI and they've at least heard of the CIA. As a result, if anything goes public, both of their spin machines will have us sliced and diced before we know what hit us. I understand you simply tried to do a friend a favor. In the past, I've done the same kind of thing myself. But this wasn't the way to do it."

There was a slight pause before Collier resumed. "Tell you what, Frank. Write up a report detailing your breach and I'll try to present it in a positive manner. I just don't want to be second-guessed at the next security review. For now, describe in your report that you were looking for potential security soft spots and you found several 'trap doors.' Hopefully administration will realize you probably prevented some eventual embarrassments by exposing weak areas."

"Thanks, boss."

Chapter VIII

CIA—ASAP

Frank Bishop wheeled his silver Mercedes convertible off the Capital Beltway onto Baltimore Avenue. Heading south, he approached the University of Maryland campus and took a series of left turns before arriving at the parking lot of an especially seedy-looking restaurant. Verdi's wasn't an old establishment, but looks were deceiving. To top it off, the place looked like a mob hangout. As Bishop pulled into the parking lot, several hefty men with extra dark sunglasses and jacket bulges arrived in very expensive cars.

Bishop grinned and surmised how ironic it would be for employees from the NSA and CIA to meet inside a joint later found to have had mob ties, all while working on the JFK assassination. Approaching the entrance, sharp aromas of pasta and garlic increased with each step. Inside, they became borderline noxious. As Bishop watched a cheerleader-esque college-age hostess, another waiter holding several enormous plates of calzone whizzed past, almost knocking him over. Then the hostess spoke.

"How many for tonight?"

"Uh, two. I'm meeting a husky 60-ish guy who probably already grabbed us a table."

"Oh, I think he may be seated. Right this way."

Wayne Schaefer was sequestered in a booth nursing a beer at a far corner of the restaurant. Bishop soon heard his booming voice.

"Frank—You're actually on time!"

Bishop joked in his low voice: "Not too loud, you'll destroy my image."

Noticing Schaefer's beer, Bishop caught a passing waiter. "I'll have a Stella, please…and let's refill my friend's while you're at it."

"Sure thing, sir."

Once the drinks arrived, Schaefer pounced. "Frank. I still have a hard time believing we may finally have an opportunity to work together."

"Wait a minute, Wayne. First, you're going to have to lay out what you're proposing."

Schaefer half stood up and scanned the room. Quaffing his beer, he proceeded to wipe foam from his upper lip, then looked directly at Bishop.

"It's about the JFK assassination. A film has surfaced that's not been seen. We just got a copy and it came from a guy we're tracking named Winston. This guy has no formal intel ties, yet his fingerprints are all over the biggest mystery of the last century. Like you found out, he's talking with the FBI. That means we have to nail down what's going on, or we're looking at another fifty years of accusations and finger-pointing on how the CIA blew the Kennedy assassination, or even worse, how we were complicit. After the FBI tampering that went down by doctoring the Zapruder film, we simply can't take a chance for the tables to be flipped on us yet again."

Bishop looked across the room before speaking wistfully. "This whole thing seems strange, doesn't it, Wayne? I mean such an old case...so high-profile...so worked over. And even after so long, it keeps coming up again."

"That's right, Frank. With all the incomplete answers, new theories are bound to continue being spun as new stuff comes out. Where you wanna start?"

"I'm still not sure if I can help you that much. But if keeping a lid on it is that important, we both understand one of the first rules of secrecy is compartmentalization. Simply realize anything we discuss is on a 'need to know basis,' especially within our respective agencies. Outside of that, the only actionable information that should get passed around is reserved for those in a position to make good use of it."

Schaefer nodded in agreement. "That's why joining forces makes sense, Frank. We'll have more communication on the stuff that really matters. In an ideal world, we could team with the FBI, but there's still too much ingrained distrust after all these years...especially on this case. Maybe the next generation can make that dog hunt," Schaefer said hopefully.

"Well, you must have something figured out, or we wouldn't be talking. The one thing I know about you, Wayne, is that you're a man of action."

Schaefer rubbed his index fingers nervously against each thumb. "Frank, make that a man of action...with a plan.

"Is this your plan, Wayne...or the agency's?"

"Mine. All mine. I had to twist arms like you wouldn't believe. And even now, it's my neck on the line."

Bishop tensed for a moment, sighed, then leaned back away from the table. "OK, fine, Wayne. Let's hear it."

"I thought you'd never ask." Schaefer's face lit up as he folded his hands together. "OK, Frank, here's the deal. As we discussed earlier, reliable surveillance shows our target is a real estate agent...as you so capably researched...a guy named Winston."

"Right."

Schaefer leaned back from the table and pondered aloud. "Real estate agent. Isn't that a great cover?"

Bishop thought for a moment before responding. "Yeah—it is pretty ingenious, come to think of it. Real estate agents often have strange hours, a lot of unpredictable, hard-to-track independent movements, plus 24/7 access to properties of all types. They also have the cachet of being licensed professionals. And to top it all off, nowadays real estate agents have criminal background checks that immediately render them non-criminals. As a result, they're automatically above suspicion."

Schaefer smiled. "Right…and we know it must be just a cover with this Ron Winston, because you confirmed he's currently under FBI protection. My guess is his background has been scrubbed clean by someone. There's no logical reason for a guy who sells houses to need federal cover. He's also apparently got a concealed carry permit. Adding it all up, this guy doesn't pass the smell test. But there's also one other thing."

"What's that?"

"Our sources confirm plenty of people want a piece of this Winston guy," Schaefer continued, sipping his beer. "Whatever he knows—about the JFK assassination anyway—is still spotty. But based on my reports alone, the guy is a walking Petri dish of criminal interest right now. He's got people trailing him from all over. I fully suspect the bureau has had an inside track all along, given his enhanced FBI protection. Anyone tied to the Kennedy caper and flying this low under the radar so long after November 22, 1963 tells me the guy must know something important."

"Agreed," Bishop replied, grasping his drink. He scooted closer to the table between them.

"So, Wayne. What's your plan?"

"We tunnel."

Bishop stared at Schaefer quizzically.

"What do you mean, 'We tunnel?'"

Schaefer sighed.

"Frank, we have less than 70 hours to resolve this. Either we strike now and find out what Winston has, or let history be re-written. Except if we don't act now, someone else will author history. I realize you're younger than me, Frank, but are you at all familiar with the history on 'Operation Gold' during the Cold War?"

"Vaguely, but I have a feeling I'm suddenly about to become a lot more familiar."

Schaefer half stood and once more scanned the room. Sitting down, he lowered his voice. "'Operation Gold' copied the success British Intelligence had with 'Operation Silver' in Austria. "

Bishop rolled his eyes. "Okay, fine. We've got gold and silver...what's next—platinum?"

Unfazed, Schaefer resumed. "In 'Operation Silver,' the Brits covertly tapped into the landline communications of the *Soviet Army* headquarters in *Vienna*. It allowed England to essentially read the Russkies' mail."

Gaining interest, Bishop spoke up. "Okay then...I guess my communist history is a tad rusty. So if that was silver, what was 'gold' about?"

"'Operation Gold' occurred in Communist East Germany when the CIA oversaw tunneling into a critical telephone junction that rested less than six feet underground. You might recall that after World War II, the city of Berlin was cut up into four sectors, each administered by the prevailing powers: France, Britain, the United States and Russia. All except the Russian sector were free. Yet where Russian territory bordered the American sector, three cables came together. We tapped into those cables and read plenty of Soviet and East German communiqués. In fact, a few of my old-timer friends were involved in that one."

"Fine. So you're proposing that we dig. Where?" Bishop asked.

"Good question. For now, two places…and we don't have much time, so the easier, the better."

"Okay. What two places?"

"Not so fast. There's one other element that wasn't involved with Operations Gold and Silver."

"What's that?"

"There's no time to monitor the situation, so we nab and grab."

"Kidnap?"

"Precisely."

"Whoa."

Bishop stared blankly.

"Your hunch better be a good one."

"It is, Frank. This one is for all of the marbles. So first, we hit the residence where our intel confirms this Winston guy lives."

"Where does he live?"

"Suburban Dallas."

"Alright," Bishop nodded. "That part's easy enough. And second?"

Schaefer smirked without saying a word.

"Wayne, what's that second place you propose to tunnel?"

"Promise not to laugh?"

"Yes."

Schaefer looked calmly at Bishop. "Offices inside the FBI."

A fine mist of beer shot out Bishop's nose. "Sorry—I promised not to laugh."

Bishop motioned to a waitress across the room. "Could I please get a few more napkins over here...and another beer?"

With composure regained moments later, Bishop looked around the room. "About that FBI office..."

"Yeah," Schaefer responded.

"What's the working plan for that?"

"Like I was saying about Operations Silver and Gold, if we drop a roving wiretap inside their communications net, we find out what they have on this Winston guy and what their plans are. If nothing else, we can defend ourselves when they start to cast blame on the CIA and eventually you guys at the NSA."

"You realize tapping into the FBI would make Watergate look like a tea party?" Bishop stated.

"Yeah. But this is about the JFK assassination," Schaefer stated matter-of-factly.

"How good's your intel on the layout for this Winston guy's house?"

Schaefer smiled. "I've got the address, maps, building plans and floorplan. Our assets close to the situation suspect the FBI has his residence bugged. But someone like you inside the NSA could confirm that. There's also apparently a roving team of agents outside, watching the place 'round-the-clock. You know the deal—the usual FBI gadgetry with remote controlled cameras...maybe even satellites. That's what makes this a perfect set-up for tunneling....and possibly some duct work."

"So this would truly be a 'nab & grab?'"

"You got it—a classic 'black bag' operation all the way."

Schaefer held his hand up and whispered. "Just a second, Frank. Here comes the next round." As the waitress walked away, Bishop appeared anxious.

"So what do we do with this Winston guy who appears to hold information on the JFK 'hit' once we snatch him?"

Taking a big breath, Schaefer rubbed the back of his neck. "That's way beyond my pay grade, Frank. But for a case like the Kennedy assassination, I could recommend a place out of country for starters. Maybe let the Israelis have a crack at him. He'd talk then."

Bishop drummed his fingers on the table. "Okay, then. How high up does this one go?"

Schaefer smiled. "Officially?"

"Yeah, officially," Bishop responded.

"Short of a subpoena, my boss is in a position to plausibly deny *everything* if there's even a bump in the road. So, along with three other team members, we're it. That makes four CIA recruits…and you—an NSA insider."

Bishop grew cautious. "So if our respective agencies are found out?"

"I can virtually guarantee department heads from both our organizations would totally disavow any knowledge of the operation."

"That's really brilliant," Bishop said, snapping his fingers. "Wayne, think of it. Government agencies can cover their tracks by simply reverting back to a spin on the old 'rogue' assassin theory, where a handful of government malcontents supposedly took out JFK."

"That's right," Schaefer agreed. "Our respective agencies can never have too many fall-guys. Besides, the CIA has long been deemed complicit to the crime, anyway, so in a sense there's very little downside. 'Spook' lore is rife with theories that imply a few CIA bad eggs, backed by the military-industrial complex, wanted to prevent the US withdrawal from Vietnam, while finishing the job Kennedy didn't get done at the Bay of Pigs. Of course, that first meant putting the White House under new management, then taking out Castro, since the Bay of Pigs invasion was such a debacle. But you're right. Even now, all these decades later, if we're caught, that same old 'rogue theory' chestnut will be used against us again by those who want to cover up the FBI's lousy job of solving the puzzle."

Bishop smiled. "I guess it can't be any worse than what already went down, back in 1963, right?"

"Precisely," Schaefer acknowledged. "What does the CIA really have to lose? We've already been implicated. And if not directly blamed for the JFK assassination, at least for a purported cover-up."

"But why do you need me and the NSA, Wayne? I mean, it might be a little harder as a CIA-only operation, but you guys have plenty of cross-training capabilities to handle this solo."

Schaefer looked resignedly at Frank. "Maybe. But aside from superior NSA monitoring capabilities, if a single agency shakes up the FBI, there'll be a lot of finger pointing. By joining forces, we're far more credible. Plus, combined we really do have better resources. If everything goes as planned, we all deserve to share the credit. Lord knows both of our agencies can use some good PR these days. And that should help us both in getting our budgets increased. Plus, if we're successful, they might decide to keep a 'war horse' like me around, instead of out to pasture." Schaefer continued, with narrowed eyes. "I'll be honest with you, Frank. I've got a personal stake in this, or I wouldn't ask anything of you. Call it payback to me for a favor I did long ago if that helps, but I haven't been treated well by my own agency these past few years. I'd like to show my 'higher-ups' how absolutely wrong they've been."

Bishop nodded. "I understand and have to admit…it isn't looking so great for my position, either. I expected to be a 'lifer' at NSA. But my last few performance reviews were overseen by managers literally half my age. And often when I detect a threat, they'll insist we don't have the personnel to pursue what I know are some pretty important intercepts."

"That's scary," Schaefer replied.

"I know," Bishop nodded. "I sure don't want another November 22nd."

Schaefer shifted in his seat before responding. "Or another 9/11, either. Frank, earlier today I received tacit 'go-ahead' for covert action. I've requisitioned the manpower, materiel and a workable plan. With an NSA employee like you on board, we'll have the bases covered. Now what we *don't* have is a lot of time. That being the case, I've arranged a meeting at 10 PM for everyone on the team. We'll be at the Grey Rabbit. It's a CIA recruiting hangout, so we can secure a quiet room and go over the operation there."

Bishop glanced at his watch as the two men rose from the table. "I have to stop at the office first. See you there at 10."

"Sure, Frank. Oh, and one other thing."

"Yeah?"

"I'll need your plan for monitoring the FBI's Dallas-Ft. Worth communications grid."

Bishop gulped. "When do you need it?"

"Yesterday."

"A few hours later at 10 PM, the Grey Rabbit pub was packed with college students on Spring Break. Bishop drove up and marveled at the brilliance of the venue. *A CIA-owned college hot-spot. Who would've imagined something like this was even possible? Certainly not during Vietnam. And what a clever place to surveill the brightest potential recruits.*

Pushing open the restaurant's heavy dark oak entrance door, Frank Bishop waded through the bustling sea of humanity. He was waved over by Wayne Schaefer in back of the establishment. Standing with him was a wiry, athletic man around 30 years old.

"Hey Frank."

"Howdy, Wayne. Who's your mentor?"

"Frank, meet Ben Childers."

"Hi, Ben. Your presence here speaks volumes about your abilities."

"I've heard some good things about you, as well, Mr. Bishop."

"Not a word of it's true," Bishop grimaced through his teeth, before breaking out into a smile. "That is, unless it involves tall, leggy blondes and plenty of Chianti."

Slapping the young man on the arm, Bishop laughed heartily. "Call me Frank."

"Frank, for my money Ben Childers is the best B & E guy around," Schaefer opined.

Bishop stroked his face and began chiding the young man. "Breaking and entering, huh? They still teach that?"

"You bet," retorted Childers. "Fundamentals will always be needed."

Schaefer pointed to Childers' nineteen inch biceps. "Ben was a Navy Seal and Purple Heart recipient in Afghanistan. An enemy sniper wounded him. When he was released, we snagged him." Schaefer glanced across the room. "But there's also another distinguished person I want you to meet, Frank."

Drink in hand, Bishop looked up as a tall, blonde woman attired in a little black dress looked their way. Before she was in audible range, Bishop motioned to Schaefer.

"You're kidding," Bishop whispered. "But just so you know, I wasn't joking about the Chianti, either."

"No kidding at all, Frank. Follow me. I'd like to introduce you to someone special. Katarina, this is Frank

Bishop. He's helping us co-ordinate our upcoming project."

Her accent was as thick as her long, blonde mane.

"So good to see you, Mr. Bishop."

Bishop smiled.

"The pleasure's all mine, believe me."

"Frank, Katarina is proficient in linguistics and small caliber weaponry."

Bishop raised his eyebrows. "A powerful combination. I'll make sure to stay on your good side."

Katarina winked. "How is it you say—keep your powder dry?"

Bishop winked back.

Schaefer began motioning to Ben Childers.

"Katarina, have you met Ben?"

"Not yet."

"Katarina, this is Ben Childers. He's our B & E guy. If needed, he'll pave a way for you to do your small arms magic."

Realizing the young woman could be packing an arsenal of weaponry immediately behind him as they worked, Childers was dumbfounded.

"She's careful, right?"

"Best we've got, Childers."

"Some covers are as good as the book," Childers grinned.

Schaefer turned to the young woman. "Katarina, would you mind telling Ben your great-grandfather's name?"

Throwing blonde locks over her shoulder, the young woman suddenly appeared embarrassed.

"What I have done, I have done on my own. But I am not so famous. Yet my great-grandfather, perhaps you have heard of him, no?"

Unsure if he was being set up for a joke, Childers cautiously took the bait. "Maybe. What's his name?"

"Mikhail Kalashnikov."

Childers looked to Schaefer. "Kalashnikov? As in the famous Soviet rifle designer?"

"Yes," Katarina replied.

"That's good enough for me," Childers said. "I'm ready to lock and load."

"Glad you're satisfied," Schaefer nodded.

"Also me," offered Katarina.

Schaefer scanned the room and saw a slender man with short dark hair enter the building. Looking to the group, Schaefer announced "There's one more person I want everyone to meet."

Jerry 'Rico' Tallerico sauntered up to Schaefer and his team. "Hey Skipper."

Schaefer lowered his voice to a whisper and glanced at each team member. "Rico's our sniper. He's battle-tested and cool under fire. That right, Rico?"

"Compared to what I saw in Afghanistan, this should be a cake walk, boss."

As a waiter passed by, Schaefer motioned him over. "I've reserved 'The Hutch' for our group and it looks like everyone has arrived. May we use it now?"

"Why yes, of course. This way, please."

Schaefer guided their coterie through the restaurant with a hooked index finger. They entered a gigantic den-like room, with walls of books, a crackling fire and a long oak table fit to seat several dozen. Silver chafing dishes were arranged on the perimeter of the room, comprising a veritable smorgasbord. Tastefully-appointed gold chandeliers emitted a distinct 'olde world' ambiance.

"Thank you," uttered Schaefer. The waiter slowly closed the room's French doors after announcing: "Please feel free to serve yourself. You can press the service button here on the wall to let me know when I may take any further orders."

"Will do," Schaefer responded as he pulled a large document from his coat jacket. He unrolled a map on the long table before the group, then drew a circle with his finger around a red "X" on the document.

"We'll eat after going over this," Schaefer announced. For our mission, here's the objective," Schaefer announced, tapping a large finger near the map's center. He glanced at his watch, before returning his attention to the map. "We have precisely 67 hours to dig through and extract the target from this location."

Childers spoke up. "Just for the sake of argument, Wayne...what if he's not there?"

Schaefer sighed. "We've got plenty of possible contingencies, Childers. But that one's among the least likely, or I wouldn't have invited any of you here. Look. I'm not going to kid you guys—this isn't going to be easy. But you'll be well-compensated for your efforts and there's also a bit of luck following us. On my way over, I just learned we've acquired immediate access to a vacant rental, two doors down. That shortens our digging distance to less than 100 feet. Best of all for this job, our rental house is big, with an unfinished basement. That'll make our tunneling work even easier."

Bishop raised his hand. "Can you walk us through the sequence, Wayne?"

"Planning is always crucial, but on this one we're also going to have to roll with the punches, especially since we're going up against counter-intelligence capabilities of the FBI. As a result, our sequencing is more like a 'best case' scenario, so progress is likely to be phased. This means much will depend on each immediate challenge and the related threat level. As an example, some of our most likely unexpected issues for the target extraction are bound to be mis-marked or unidentified underground barriers, like sewer and water lines, at least to start."

Schaefer pulled folded sheets from his breast jacket. "Pass these around," Schaefer said. "We've got equipment being set up as we speak. First up is construction of a phony fence."

Schaefer pointed at his map. "See the straight brown line, everyone? That's where the fence is going in. It'll be 50 feet long. That fence construction should help draw attention from any of our recon activity. Just as important, it'll deflect our subterranean noise away from the target house. We have it timed to prevent detection by FBI agents staked out on the roof and environs. Once we're directly under the target house, we dig upward. Then, in the middle of the night, we access the crawlspace. From there, it's spiriting the guy out of there, using the same way out as how we got in."

"You got a floor plan of the place, Skipper?" Rico queried.

"Right here," Schaefer exclaimed confidently, patting his hand on a rolled up paper on the table before him. "We can go over it next, if you'd like. Just remember the crawl space will be located in the absolute center of the home, on the main floor inside the pantry. So when you pop your heads up into the target house, be careful for possible shelving. I don't want to hear about anyone getting knocked out by a large jar of spaghetti sauce. Looks like you've got a question, Katarina."

"What will be used to debilitate any secondary targets? Gas, flash-bang grenades, or stun guns?

"Excellent question," Schaefer responded. "Actually, it'll be none of those, at least initially. Instead, Rico will use thorazine darts from a side yard to temporarily neutralize any FBI roof dwellers. The trick he'll have is to bunch his hits so that once one guy goes down, the others don't scramble. We've made arrangements to have the dosages pre-calibrated. A few real time NSA satellites, courtesy of Frank here, provided some nice enhanced photos. They give us a pretty good idea of their sizes. As a former sniper myself, I gotta tell ya, those shots have to be timed just right, or it could cause those rooftop sentries serious injuries in a fall. And the less lasting damage to our FBI brethren, the better. Thankfully, Rico is more than up to the job."

Rico broke in. "Yeah, given the close range, I'll have both the cartridge gunpowder and dosages cut in half, then 'double tap' 'em with the chlorpromazine while they're taking a break—either while sitting, taking a snooze, or maybe relieving themselves in the bushes."

Schaefer resumed, pointing at the map. "As for the primary target, he gets it with gas."

Katarina looked perplexed. "Why gas?"

"Katarina, all our target needs to do is hear an opening door or squeaking board as we approach and he could be on the phone to the police or his FBI handlers. We also don't know if any bodyguards will be inside the residence. So the safest way is to assume there are others with him. Gas can handle that and it's quiet. Anyway, once we're under the house, the HVAC ducts look like a piece of cake for insertion. A few canisters of well-placed halothane with a radio-controlled activator should do the trick. House plans provide us with the square footage, so we have a general sense of dosage calibration. Electricity will be cut just before to prevent the air conditioning unit from cleaning out our 'magic dust.' And thankfully our recon shows no signs this Winston guy leaves his windows open at night. Otherwise, that'd make gas ineffective. Anyway, we'll need to wear masks on entering. If the target acts up once we're in there, he gets an injection of diazepam. Either way, he'll be snoozing on his way out."

"Do you have a physical description on the target, so we can make sure to ID the guy?"

"Glad you asked, Ben." Schaefer began handing each team member a manila folder. "Here's a dossier on Ron Winston. It includes the usual intel. Height, weight, age, plus plenty of photos of this guy, since he's a self-promoting real estate agent. Now unless there are any more questions, I suggest you all eat, then get some shuteye. We'll meet up at a location I'll forward to you by 0600 in the morning and at that time you'll be provided with our exact tactical sequence. Make sure to study a copy of the house layout so you can all memorize it for our ingress and egress. That's it for now."

As the group later broke up, Bishop walked with Schaefer to the parking lot. "Wayne, I have a bit more information for you."

"What's it about, Frank?"

"I've been thinking about the best way to tap into the FBI's computer system. Our chance of tunneling as done in 'Operation Gold' and 'Operation Silver' is simply too risky. Besides, the bureau is compartmentalized now, so what I'll need to do is work on a 'roving' basis."

"How's that work?"

"I need to monitor communications to defend against eavesdropping during our operation and also hopefully listen in on any of their chatter. But rather than do any digging, my main job will be moving around in cyber-space for any activity tipping off our operation."

"Sounds great. Let's do it."

"There's only one problem."

"Problem? What is it?"

"I'll first have to defeat the FBI's encryption."

"How long could that take?"

"Depends. By linking a string of super-computers together, I can crunch a lot of data. I'll start tonight. If I get lucky, I may even find a 'trap door' or two."

"Trap door?"

"Programming lingo. Sometimes an encryption programmer will leave himself a way in, just in case he loses the "key" necessary to break a code. It's rarely obvious, but I only need one."

Schaefer shook his head. "I'm glad you're on our side, Frank. Catch you in the morning."

By 9:00 AM, Wayne Schaefer reconnoitered his crew inside a remote, vacant government warehouse. Prying hard with a screeching crowbar at one edge of a huge wooden crate, he popped off the lid. Digging his hand inside the straw-like packing material, Schaefer pulled out a stack of neatly-packed handguns. Smiling as he realized Bailey's follow-through, Schaefer racked the slide on a brand-new Heckler & Koch 9mm semi-automatic pistol and passed it to the man standing next to him.

"Contingency plans dictate what we'll be using, Rico…in case someone tries to take out our target…or us, as we close in. H & K is among the finest. You'll appreciate the smooth action on these."

Jerry 'Rico' Tallerico accepted the weapon with both hands. Fingering the cold metal, he closed one eye, gazed down the weapon's gun sight, smiled and tucked it snugly into his waistband. "You know smooth is what I do best, boss. And while I'm more of a rifle guy, this'll do fine in a pinch."

Schaefer grinned. "Speaking of rifles, I special-ordered some nice pieces for your longer shots, Rico. Remind me before we leave. Since you're the sniper, I definitely want you to have first pick."

As an enlisted man during Operation Desert Storm, Jerry 'Rico' Tallerico had arrived in Kuwait to skies black from oil well fires, courtesy of Saddam Hussein. Recognized as a shockingly accurate sniper, it had been Rico's job to take out enemy combatants within 1,000 metres of any Kuwaiti oil rig. He even sandbagged that distance a bit, for his 'kill zone' was reputed to be

1,800 metres or more, depending on the weather and if he'd had his morning coffee—it smoothed his nerves, thereby improving his already-stellar marksmanship. While serving overseas he'd piled up a few medals.

After receiving severe shell-shock from a roadside bomb, Rico went stateside. For several years, he bummed around the US and eventually tried to make a go of it as a police officer. During his probationary period, Rico was discharged after breaking a resistant suspect's arm during what began as a routine traffic stop. Hunting for work months later, Schaefer's phone call came at the perfect time. Rico was grateful, needed the money and was always calm under fire. Schaefer appreciated the fact that Rico was truly battle-tested. Looking around the remote warehouse, Schaefer cleared his throat, then lowered his voice.

"Alright. Listen up." The room turned silent.

"You all know we have work to do and not much time. Let me first say I'm glad each one of you is here, especially after our late night. Like I've always said, I'll never knowingly let you down. I simply ask for your best. Now let's walk through the mission."

Schaefer paced a few feet and turned around to face his crew. "I know you've now all met, but I'll continue to make comments to remind everybody about your abilities, until you all know everyone's strengths. I want you to think like a team and that means knowing who's best qualified for a given task under changing conditions."

"So let me briefly re-introduce each of you. Everyone say 'Hi' to Rico. He'll be our long distance gunner. If the situation gets hot or we're simply dealing with a long shot, we go to Rico. Everybody clear? Of course, if you're in a tight spot and Rico's gone, you do what you can. But that isn't an excuse to 'hot dog,' since we'll be in continual radio contact. Just keep me informed about any meaningful variations in the mission. Now, next up is Ben Childers. For those who don't remember, he's both our explosives and B & E guy."

Childers responded with a wide grin. "Detonations made to order, huh, Boss?"

"That's right, Ben. 'Just blow and go.' People, when it comes to anything we need decimated, Ben is just the guy to do it. Now for those of you who don't know much about explosives, let's just say that while Ben is a great guy, he's NOT someone you'd better be slapping on the back—especially when he's carrying a backpack loaded with plastic explosive. You both might end up on the ceiling."

Schaefer looked around the room.

"Katarina? There you are. For those of you who haven't heard, she comes from a long line of engineers. But not the kind to draw up plans for building bridges. She's a weapons engineer specializing in small caliber firearms and speaks seven languages fluently. So if you yahoos have a problem with your sidearm, rifle, or in a pinch, with a fuse—talk with Katarina. Weaponry engineering is part science, part art…and you might say she's been trained by the best. Right, Katarina?"

"Thank you very much."

"Last, but not least everyone, say hello again to Frank Bishop. An NSA insider, Frank is our intel man. For any communication issues like satellite link-ups, web-cams, counter-surveillance, bugsweeping, wiretaps, monitoring and the like, Frank's our guy. He's also the one who will be allowing us to read the FBI's mail. Frank, care to say a few words?"

"Thanks, Wayne," Frank Bishop said, scanning the room. "It's a pleasure to work with you all. I know you must be incredibly capable under fire, because Wayne's a true professional and demanding as they come. I'll be dealing mainly with counter-intelligence tactics throughout the operation. This allows me to warn you if anyone is monitoring our activities, in real time. I want to underscore that I'll be providing all of you with roaming multi-frequency surveillance capability. We'll go over details later, but for now you can feel confident that your communications are protected. In the unlikely event you believe your location is compromised, there won't be any guesswork. I'll be in a position to know and will be in direct contact with each of you as I'm monitoring all related chatter."

"Frank," Schaefer interjected. "Since the FBI's resources are a big question mark on this particular mission, care to give us a hint about the reliability of your monitoring of the bureau? I'd hate to have them get the drop."

"Sure," Bishop said. "I just tapped into one of the FBI's more vulnerable communications channels and was surprised, since it's rarely used anymore. But during my surveillance around the target house, I picked up a frequency hopping transmission. As a sidenote, it it was invented by none other than Hollywood starlet Hedy Lamarr. At NSA we have incredible code-breaking capabilities for that kind of thing."

"Care to explain frequency hopping?" Childers asked.

"Sure. Frequency hopping started back during the Second World War. Instead of operating constantly on a single frequency, it was learned that communications could be nicely encrypted by having both transmitter and receiver 'jump' to different frequencies quickly at the same time. We're talking fractions of a second here. So unless you know the frequencies as they rapidly change, you can't intercept the communique□."

Bishop took a deep breath and continued. "However, a receiver in synch with the transmitter can pick up the signal nicely. With a standard scanner, you'd not likely notice the existence of a transmission using frequency hopping, nor be able to pinpoint the location. Monitoring the hopping sequence frequencies would result only in a burst of noise of say, 1/12 to 1/50 of a second in duration. Best of all, my monitoring of the FBI will occur as it happens. So if anything within miles of our operation is talked about, you'll all get an immediate 'heads up' in your earpiece. That's because I can hear THEM hear US. And unlike certain FBI communication modes, *our* transmissions are far more secure."

"Thanks, Frank. Now unless there are any questions, we've all got an 0200 flight departure for Dallas in just a few hours. I've set up each one of you with your own lodging and vehicle there, but feel free to sleep on the plane. See you at our pre-arranged destination."

Chapter IX

Mob Rule

Ron Winston heard something whiz past his ear as he turned the suburban Dallas corner during an early morning walk. At 4:30 AM, few people were usually around. That made it easy for Winston to relax and temporarily forget some of his more demanding clients. Were it not for the ricochet off the brick wall behind him, Winston might have mistaken the rifle shot for a caffeinic bumblebee. Winston dropped and rolled on the ground, bracing himself against wheels of a dumpster.

"Silencers? What next?"

Once more a target, Winston scurried in retreat to the alley behind him. His mind reeled through the usual list of President Kennedy's murder suspects Mackey said had been bandied about for decades. Now all these years later, someone seemed to want Winston dead, too.

"These guys are playing for keeps," Winston whispered to himself, out of breath.

"But who are they working for? The Mob? CIA? Russians? Cubans?" Winston was relieved to realize one ingredient was not part of this rich assassination stew: "At least I'm not being pursued on orders from L.B.J."

Approaching the alley's opposite end, Winston slowed his pace to a jaunt. Crouching low, he peered left, then right.

Zwing!

The round grazed his shirtsleeve and he ducked reflexively.

"High power, that one."

Retreating further, his head banged against the nearby building. Given the second shot's angle, there was no way the same gunman could have fired both. Since dawn hadn't yet arrived, Winston realized he still had a few things in his favor. "That is, unless they've got night vision scopes," he relented, then exhaled deeply. "This doesn't look good."

Winston was cornered and his adversaries clearly knew their weapons. Yet having twice missed, were they simply playing 'cat and mouse' to scare him with some kind of a warning? Winston made sure to remain inside the alley, listening for any approaching footsteps. With his own handgun locked in a car trunk blocks away, Winston considered his dwindling options, then rattled off prospective tactics from a mental list.

"One, I stay put and eventually get nailed as they wait me out before gradually closing in. Two, I make a break from either end of the alley and give only one shooter a clear shot. Or, three…" he thought, glancing up. "Look heavenward."

Winston's last option was not entirely religious. Making it work meant first reaching, then climbing the fire escape taunting him overhead. The leap was considerable. But soon hanging from the escape's bottom rung, Winston began swinging his legs in unison. On the third try, he gained enough momentum to grasp a rail above using both feet.

Ka-chang. Tinkle.

A target shooter himself, Winston recognized that sound of an ejected bullet casing hitting pavement. Judging from where the most recent bullet landed, one shooter had found a new angle.

"Great. They're repositioning and that guy is close," he murmured. "Of all the times for the streets to be empty. Doesn't anyone else hear these guys? And where's a police officer when you need one, anyway?"

Realizing he'd have to completely change position, Winston simply let go in a free fall. As his tingling heels hit unforgiving asphalt, his knees buckled, partially absorbing the remaining shock. Rolling on his side, his body throbbed from the waist down. "This isn't working," he winced. There was no time to shake off the pain. Seconds left him like rope on a tossed anchor. Winston realized his final hope was a sprint covering the football-field distance to his Saab and the weapon inside. Heels still stinging, he bolted. Darting and weaving in a determined and zig-zag pattern, he reached full steam mid-way to the vehicle.

Ka-phew.

Cement chips penetrated flesh just below his left knee. Winston crumpled to the ground before pulling himself to a crouch behind a lamp post base. Catching breath between sentences, he told himself: "They're not losing accuracy with distance. So why don't they just finish me off?"

Ka-chang.

"A lucky miss."

Lifting his pantleg to assess his knee, Winston realized there were at least a few seconds between reports as both shooters re-acquired their sight pictures. Winston scampered the final distance across the war zone of pavement and found cover by leaning against his vehicle. Desperately grasping his car keys, he draped one arm against a corner bumper and sucked in air. With his back pressing up against a car tire, Winston punched the automatic trunk opener inside his pocket. He smiled on hearing the comforting *'Thunk.'*

"Just in time," he exhaled, grateful to be close to a weapon and with decent cover. Winston tore inside the open trunk. Hurriedly digging, he reached for the weapon's square grey carrying case. Inside, it held his final, if meager, line of defense, a .380 Sig Sauer semi-automatic. Teeth clenched, Winston tried to convince himself he still had one option.

"Ten-to-one I'm up against bolt actions. Well, I may be outgunned given their accuracy...but if I'm going down, then they're coming with me."

Moments later came a loud *'SPLASH'* as the Saab's tempered rear windshield vaporized. Winston extracted his handgun from the case and snatched two loaded ammo clips. Quickly examining the weapon, he was determined to answer the last shot.

"Incredible," he whispered to himself during the sudden stillness. "As a real estate agent, I get a concealed carry permit to deal with mean dogs in bad parts of town. Instead, I'm shot at by two-legged ones in the high rent district."

Winston slammed a full ammo clip into the Swiss weapon's handle and smartly racked the slide to chamber a round. He took a long, quiet breath and wondered aloud: "These clowns are using a lot more firepower than *any* pistol load," Winston reminded himself.

Winston was outgunned in more ways than one. Worst of all was his handgun's reduced accuracy and range compared to a long barreled rifle. Winston's pistol provided far less reach than what the thugs had at their disposal. Best known as a '9mm short,' his Sig was of the same caliber as its fatter NATO-approved cousin, but with a much shorter cartridge. This meant reduced gunpowder and less 'punch' than a standard 9mm round.

Looking at his lone back up ammo clip, Winston suddenly realized just how bad his odds really were. For in addition to his carrying a less accurate short barreled handgun, he remembered opting for 'safety' ammo, now making for a dire situation. He'd been told safety slugs were a great 'urban load' to prevent gunshots from penetrating walls and hitting nearby innocents. Yet Winston's safety slugs were no match in range or accuracy against bad guys wielding high-power rifles. Designed to fragment on impact, his slugs stood little chance of penetrating obstacles, or any bullet-proof vests possibly worn by his assailants

During the sudden quiet, Winston leveled with himself, muttering: "This doesn't look good." Suddenly all hell broke loose, with Winston on the receiving end of sustained rapid fire spitting under the car's chassis.

Budda-budda-budda-budda.

"Now they've gone fully auto." The barrage continued, as the echo of automatic weapons fire off nearby buildings nearly deafened him. Now leaning hard against a rear wheel, Winston looked around and heard a high-pitched wheezing sound confirm his tires were shot out.

"Terrific. So much for me leaving now"

Out of nowhere, Winston heard two rapid muffled reports, then silence. *It sounds like a freaking war zone,* he thought. Moments later, a faint siren sounded. In less than a minute the shriek was deafening. A lone patrolman pulled up to the curb, blue and red lights throwing a kaleidoscope on the street and a nearby window as night retreated. The officer left his vehicle, hand tense on his sidearm. Winston realized his own handgun remained in plain view. The officer reflexively drew his weapon. Standing with both hands extended, the patrolman held what appeared to be a sizeable black semi-automatic, then barked "Freeze."

Shell-shocked from playing target minutes earlier, Winston didn't move.

"Lay the weapon down slowly, mister."

"Are you talking to me?"

"That's right. Now lay the weapon down *very* slowly."

"Yes sir."

Winston opened his palm and heard the gun land on pavement.

"Back away from the weapon. Keep moving. Keep moving. Now stop and sit on the ground with your hands in the air."

Winston felt a firm grip on the back of his belt. Suddenly he was standing on his feet.

"Can I see some I.D. here?"

"Sure, officer." Winston clumsily reached for the wallet in his back pocket.

"Slow, mister...SLOW."

Winston produced his black eelskin wallet and handed it to the officer. As a second patrol car arrived, the first officer announced firmly: "Place both hands behind your back."

Winston complied and heard the 'click' of handcuffs.

"Come with me and sit in the car."

Winston couldn't believe his ears. "Wait a minute officer. What are you doing? I was being shot a by two guys with rifles. Aren't you going to go after them?"

"One thing at a time while we sort this out. Watch your head getting inside."

The patrolman holstered his own weapon, then looked down at Winston sitting in the police car. "I was dispatched to investigate shots fired. You can tell me all about it. But first, understand you're under arrest. You have the right to remain silent. Anything you say can and will be used against you in a court of law. You have the right to speak to an attorney and to have an attorney present during any questioning. If you cannot afford an attorney, one will be provided for you at government expense. Do you understand these rights?"

"Yes, but I've done nothing wrong."

The deputy began thumbing through Winston's wallet, with his elbow pressed firmly on what Winston noticed was a Glock .40 caliber semi-automatic.

At least he's holstered his weapon, Winston thought, relieved. The look on the officer's face was filled with disgust.

"So exactly what are you doing with a handgun out in the open?"

"I have a permit."

"What type of permit?"

"Concealed carry. It's right there in my wallet."

"What kind of carry?"

"Concealed."

"I rest my case," snarled the officer. "What exactly did you think you were doing?"

"Trying to stay alive. I was being shot at."

"This some kind of a drug turf war?"

"I don't do drugs."

"Stay put."

Turning on his black-booted heel to confer with the other officer, the patrolman strode to his vehicle and spoke for a moment on his police radio. A few minutes later, he sauntered back to Winston.

"Out of the car."

Winston readily complied.

"Now turn around."

Unlocking the handcuffs, he handed back Winston's identification accompanied with a pink citation.

"It's a good thing you don't have a criminal history and part of your file in my computer is tagged 'confidential.' Otherwise I'd take you in and cite you for a lot more than brandishing. We had reports of at least one man on a rooftop with what may have been a rifle, so apparently part of your story checks out. What's this all about?"

"Like I told you, I've done nothing wrong."

"Want some good advice, Mr. Winston? Leave the gun-slinging to professionals. You'll save yourself a mess of trouble. Otherwise, somebody's bound to get hurt. Oh, and one more thing."

"What's that?"

"Be polite to the judge at your hearing. He doesn't appreciate reckless behavior...*or* a reckless attitude."

"Sure thing, officer."

Winston walked angrily over to his decimated vehicle. "That was my favorite car...what am I going to tell my insurance company? I better call Dennis."

Winston pushed the autodial on his cell phone. "Law office of Dennis Worth."

"Dennis, please."

"One moment."

"Dennis here."

"Dennis—Ron Winston. You wouldn't believe what just happened to me."

"Oh really? You wouldn't believe what just happened to *me*."

"What's that?"

"My office was broken into. Ransacked."

"Anything taken?"

"Only your files. Nothing else."

"What does that mean?"

"Smells like spy agency dirty tricks to me, Ron."

"Dennis, at least *your* car still runs."

"What happened?"

"Somebody used it for target practice…I better go, I've got to call for a tow."

Chapter X

Photo Finish

Hours before the operation, Wayne Schaefer mulled his team's assignments for each phase of their undertaking. Later as he slept, a premonition-filled dream had his entire crew lured into a trap. Once ensnared, a shoot-out ensued. The dream had Schaefer's team outnumbered five to one and in it, every team member died. This nightmare now had him wide awake. Soon, Schaefer was involved in an encrypted conversation with team member Ben Childers.

"Ben. It's Wayne."

"Wha.....Hello?"

"Ben. I know it's midnight, but I strongly believe we need an earlier operation commencement. Our new meetup time at the base house will be 0100. We'll need time to reach the target house, so Zero Hour for actually launching our target extraction is officially changed to 0230. If any of our prior communiqués have been compromised, we'll now have the advantage. Can you meet me at the safe house early?"

Wiping sleep from his face, Ben Childers spoke haltingly.

"Um...yeah, sure. I'll be there. Still park three blocks away, according to plan?"

"Right. And if you'll contact Katarina right away, I'll call Frank and Rico. Just make sure you're encrypted."

"Will do, Boss."

Ron Winston tossed restlessly in his bed. Reaching over, he grabbed the phone and hit autodial.

"Suze."

"Ron?"

"It's me. How are you?"

"I *was* sleeping. Is something wrong?"

"I just had an awful dream about the shootout I mentioned to you this morning."

"Dream? What happened?"

"Let's just say it didn't end as well as what I've experienced in real life. But I'm not paranoid anymore. Now I realize people truly *are* out to get me."

"This must be so difficult for you, Ron."

"Having you on the phone sure helps. Plus, I was told they've got my house surrounded with FBI agents. At least for tonight, it should be very secure around here."

"FBI agents? I should say. How are you coping at work?"

"My clients are doing fine. It's just that at night, when everything gets quiet, I start wondering why you and I haven't seen each other more."

"Oh I miss you, too, Ron. I can't wait to see those cute dimples of yours when you smile. Part of this is my fault, with my parents and all. Let's make time this weekend. How about Saturday *and* Sunday?"

"But what about your parents?"

"Mom said they'll be gone."

"All weekend?"

"All weekend."

"Great—I feel better already. I'll have you all to myself, then."

"It's a date. Hey, I have an idea…"

"Better be romantic."

"Oh, it is…how about us heading over to Grapevine for some wine-tasting?"

"That's sounds terrific. I'll set it up and see what the wineries have planned."

"Okay."

"Love ya, Suze."

"I love you too, Ron."

###

Ben Childers exited his assigned vehicle at 12:50 AM and walked three blocks through sultry Dallas air. He knocked twice slowly at the door of a suburban rental house with a dim exterior porch light on. The door cracked open an inch. Upon whispering the code "I'm here, good fellow," Childers was swiftly ensconced inside. Frank Bishop greeted Childers with a smile, but no slap on his explosive-laden backpack.

Childers' friendly voice broke the early morning quiet. "Hi, Frank."

"Childers—alright. It's great to see you. And on time, no less. Thanks for making the earlier start. This should give us some extra breathing room."

"Everything else according to plan, Frank?" Childers asked.

"Roger on that," said Bishop. "I'll be up here monitoring communications in case anything funky goes down. I've got this attic wired with ultra sensitive antennae and am monitoring all channels with a series of connected computers. I also set up half a dozen micro-cameras surrounding the target house. They could come in handy if the FBI decides to do anything radio-free."

"So you want me to wait here at the base house until the tunnel's dug?"

"Exactly, Childers. The Skipper's setting up underground now and Rico's in the process of taking out sentries near the target house as we speak. Once the underground passageway is clear, you'll get the word. After you set up the gas charges and enter the target house for our 'nab and grab,' it's then a matter of hightailing it back here, then splitting up according to plan."

A muffled voice called out beneath them. "Ben— we're under here. Use the small ladder."

Moseying into an adjoining bedroom, Childers crouched down and lowered himself into the cool crawlspace. There was no more than five feet of headroom under the home. As he began to walk beneath the house, Childers hunched over to keep from banging his head. He was greeted by a hard-hatted Wayne Schaefer in overalls, who held a schematic map in one hand and an unlit cigar clenched in his teeth. Off to one corner he could see long-legged Katarina in snug green camo sweats, her hair back in a French braid. Childers sidled up to Schaefer, lowered his voice and nodded toward the corner.

"Seems kind of cramped under here, but with her around, I don't mind."

Puffing on his unlit cigar, Schaefer seemed pre-occupied but chuckled in agreement.

"Yeah, I know what you mean. But don't worry, kid. For now, the hydraulic earth punch will do the heavy work and give us all a bit more breathing room."

"Earth punch?"

Schaefer sighed, pushed his hardhat back and pointed to a large machine with blinking lights located mid-way against one of the cement walls.

"Right. It's basically a four by six foot long spiral corkscrew. Bores a perfectly cylindrical hole, easily widened by rotating the auger. Pierces through layers of dirt and even concrete…though that takes longer. Needs a special attachment for that, too. Anyway, when we make a passageway through soil, whatever isn't pulled out is compressed against the tunnel walls. That minimizes loose dirt. And since it's hydraulic, it's pretty quiet. Nothing pneumatic. But I had some help with our engineers for enhanced noise and vibration abatement. Once it starts up, they'll pipe sound and exhaust away from here and into a baffle chamber. The exhaust eventually gets pushed out the chimney above us. To ensure we're extra quiet to anyone above ground, we've hampered any remaining sound with acoustical diffusers. Should keep the neighborhood peaceful, huh?"

"Yeah—at least compared to the plastic explosive I usually use," Childers laughed. Schaefer pulled his hardhat off, ran a hand over the sweat beads on his forehead, then plopped it back on as he re-focused.

"So I've heard. Anyway, as we near our target in the next hour or so, he should stay asleep." Schaefer's hands moved deftly as he described their subterranean approach. "The main thing is that as we approach the target house, we get *under* the foundation. Then we work our way *in*, well past the foundation wall. After that, we work *up*. From there, it should be a piece of cake...once we tear through a little plastic, anyway."

"A little plastic?"

"Yeah. The black vapor barrier usually found in the crawl space. It keeps moisture out of the house." Schaefer pointed at Childers. "Then, you...being our 'gas guy,' you'll get in there to fill the ventilation system with 'happy vapors' before we go in for the target extraction. One other thing."

"What's that, Skipper?" Childers asked.

"On each of your hardhats is both a light and a mini-camera. Bishop rigged me up with a hand-held computer where throughout the mission I'll be able to see what you're all doing in real time. Every hardhat carries a GPS chip, too."

"Whoa," Childers responded.

"It should help me help you, so if you have questions about what you're to do, just make sure your light is on."

"Will do, Skipper," said Rico.

Hunched to avoid hitting his head on overhead beams, Childers walked to one side under the house and marveled at the corkscrew-device being prepared nearby. He rubbed his chin. "Ingenious."

Schaefer pressed a finger against his earpiece. "Are you guys ready to begin boring?" He then looked over to give Childers and Katarina a 'thumbs-up.' Mouthing the words "Okay. Good to go," Schaefer began the countdown as two beefy, blue jump-suited men adjusted their headsets and donned gloves.

"T-minus ten seconds."

Like a concert maestro, Schaefer raised a hand and waved it back and forth as if he were a human metronome. The two man drill team watched him over their shoulders. Each time his hand moved, his lips followed in synch.

"Nine. Eight. Seven. Six. Five. Four. Three. Two. One."

On cue, the earth shook quietly. As the drilling commenced, Childers walked back to the tunnel-digging contraption and observed the two jump-suited operators. One man appeared to act as an 'aimer,' guiding the large drill's direction from side to side. The other was directly behind the machine, operating switches. Both wore hard hats. Even through their jump-suits they looked like body builders. Schaefer's entire team said nothing, assuming the men were trusted CIA covert ops agents. The resultant tidy round tunnel was large enough to crawl through. Every few minutes drilling would stop, then a team member would take turns crawling ahead to assess progress. Less than an hour later, Schaefer heard an exhilarated Katarina through his earpiece.

"We are close. It should be straight up from here."

Still chewing on his now-disgusting cigar, Schaefer walked over to Childers and hiked up his overalls. "You about ready?"

"Yep. Soon as the drill team gets back here, I'll prepare to plant the gas. Then we're off and running."

Schaefer smiled as he pushed the hardhat off his forehead. "I've never been in on your end of it before, Ben. You B & E guys have one tough job. Aside from my sniper work years ago, now I'm more like the guy who packs a parachute for the one who jumps."

Childers was his usual low-key self. "Yeah, it can get hairy, that's for sure. Think it'll be long before they reach the crawl-space?"

"Unless there's a surprise and we hit an unsuspected cement slab, I'd say five minutes, tops."

"Just say the word and I'm ready."

Childers strolled over to one corner of the base house's crawlspace and opened what looked like a large fishing tackle box. Whipping out a pair of rubber gloves, he stuffed them inside his pocket, then strapped on an ultra-thin bulletproof vest, just in case. He next donned tennis shoes and a miner's helmet. Last, he slid two large plastic-encased hypodermic syringes into the bandolier across his chest. Checking his wireless microphone, Childers heard Katarina whisper over the radio device in his ear.

"Ben. They say the earth just got nice and soft. Hold on."

There was a brief pause.

"Foxtrot Jackpot. We just broached the crawlspace entry into the target house. Ben, we're in the right spot—it won't be long before you can start heading this way now. They're ready for you to plant the gas charges as soon as you see the drillers exit back to your end."

The dirt-encrusted duo returned a few minutes later on all fours, dragging their now largely-dismantled boring device from the tunnel. Under the corkscrew-like machine was a shield pulled with rope, now used as a metal sled. Childers got down on his knees and began crawling the other way through the cavern in a half crouch. "This never gets any easier," he told himself. "I must be getting old."

Sixty feet in, Childers knew there was no turning back. He was now about as far from the base house as the target house. Even with the coal-miner's light on his helmet, the tunnel was dark, damp, dirty and cramped. And while earth was compressed against the tunnel walls, the burrow was made quickly and without structural support, so a lethal cave-in was a distinct possibility. Several times as Childers moved along, the surrounding earth above groaned as he passed through. Childers activated his transmitter and spoke softly.

"You read me, Skipper?"

"Roger that, Ben," Schaefer responded. "The boring team made two entry holes. The first hole veers to your right at a very obvious Y. That tunnel goes under the cement foundation of the target house and leads to a heating duct, perfect for planting your gas charges. But the ductwork there is in such a cramped space that it prevents you from using that as an access point to crawl under the house to reach the pantry. The drillers said it's just too tight for anybody to get through there. So once you're done planting your charges, be careful on your way back to access the second entry hole. That'll bring you much closer to the pantry access under the house. I understand the part to be careful about is a stubborn tree root toward the distal end of that tunnel. It'll snag your privates if you don't rise up a bit."

"Man, I don't need that. Thanks for telling me, Skipper. It's already plenty miserable enough in here."

After a steep descent through noticeably cooler earth under the home's cement foundation, Childers noticed the cave made a sudden turn upward.

"Finally I get to stretch a little," Childers whispered, searching for furnace ductwork. "There."

Childers dug into his carry pack. With his razor-sharp commando knife, he sliced into grey tape along the metal duct's seam. Prying ductwork apart with rubber gloves and a screwdriver-like tool, Childers slipped several gas charges inside. He rapidly patched over the slice with several pieces of fingerprint-resistant duct tape and backed away.

Schaefer was next to break radio silence. "Ben. The hole-boring crew set up a low-level light below the crawlspace opening. It's hanging on a rope there for you. Just make sure you pocket it so it's not left behind."

Moments later came a response. "Roger that. I'll keep an eye out for the light, Skipper."

Childers turned around, pointed his radio igniter at the duct under the house. Counting "One, two, three," he pressed hard on the remote button.

Childers scurried back into the tunnel, then made a beeline to the second access hole. That took him once more under the home's cement foundation wall, then through the crawlspace to eventually meet the others. Darkness began to evaporate as Childers saw light streaming down on what he realized was a staging area in the crawlspace directly under the pantry. Through his earpiece, Ben Childers heard Schaefer's hushed voice addressing him.

"Katarina can now see your helmet light, Ben. Rico joined her and they both followed you until you peeled off to plant your charges. While you were working there, they then went straight to the staging area under the pantry. Get ready for 'heads up.' Once you work your way into the cavity under the pantry, the others will be there to help you in."

Several minutes later, someone tossed a thick, white velvety cord several feet below the crawlspace dirt, hitting Childers on his miner's helmet.

"Geez...some 'heads-up.' Must've been Rico."

"Slide some rope through the loop, then sit inside it," came radio instructions in a hushed tone. We'll pull at the count of three."

"One…Two…Threeee," came the whispered warning.

In seconds, Childers flopped onto a thin sheet of black plastic below the house crawl space. He breathed in deeply, appreciating the fresher air under the house.

"I must be getting claustrophobic in my old age."

"Great job," Schaefer intoned via transmitter. "Now we begin. Childers…you have your house schematic?"

"Memorized," Childers responded, patting his chest pocket. "I'll look at it only if I space out."

"We're not too worried about minor noise now," Schaefer said. "Especially since the bedrooms are upstairs and my detonation pulse monitor shows your 'knock-out gas' was activated in the heating ducts almost 15 minutes ago. If our target isn't fast asleep when you show up, he'll be very groggy."

"How about the guys on the roof?" Childers asked Rico. "Taken care of?"

"10-4," Rico responded. "They're in dreamland—all three of 'em. Everything went according to plan. This new generation of night vision scopes makes it a piece of cake. Plus, none of the unfriendlies on the roof rolled off. Best of all, I hightailed it out of there and no one saw me."

"Any animals inside the house?"

"No records of dog ownership, Childers," Schaefer said. "We researched dog licensing and reconnoitered the house in advance. But Rico's carrying some tasty treats and a magnum stun gun if our intel is incomplete."

Childers knew the next answer, but asked just to be certain. "Skipper, are we able to absolutely confirm the absence of an alarm?"

"Yeah," Schaefer responded. "The house had an alarm connected to a rapid response monitoring service. I had Frank silence it."

"Alright," said Childers.

As team members stood assembled under the target house's pantry, Schaefer moved to one corner under the base house and spoke softly into a microphone attached to his ear: "Skipper to Team Alpha at target house—we're ready and preparing to move."

"Roger that," Bishop stated flatly from the base house's attic. "All monitoring systems functional. We are clear."

"Everyone enter slowly and quietly, just like we planned," Schaefer said.

"Childers—you're first. Make sure you gassed him good. Then next up, Katarina. You check for any extraneous in-house security systems like animals and Rico will be right behind you. Even though the target should be sound asleep, we're not taking chances. Since our target's got a concealed carry permit, we can't be too careful with this guy."

Schaefer took a deep breath. "Childers, remember—you're playing clean-up. No evidence *anywhere*. Count the booties and gloves to make sure you have them *all* before you leave. And Rico—you've got the light wand and will bring up the rear. Make sure every possible print and smudge of dirt is wiped *clean*. Remember, everyone: First thing as you leave the pantry and descend back under the house, peel off your jumpsuits and booties. Then place both in the box on your right. Last person out grabs 'em all. Even though you're wearing gloves and foot coverings, I don't want a trace left behind. This operation will be scrutinized by the best— the bureau has some keen operators."

Schaefer rubbed his chin, then smiled. "Now, if everybody's good to go, synchronize your watches to 0230 hours in fifteen seconds. Then put on your gas masks and let's do it."

Looking at his watch, Schaefer whispered "Okay, then." A few moments later he questioned his crew: "Night vision glasses on? Gas masks secure?"

Hearing everyone assent in unison, Schaefer whispered: "Then here you go. Four...three...two...one. Now!"

Childers opened the door from the pantry as the team silently accessed the home. "All-*right*," Childers whispered gleefully into his microphone. "Carpet—just like we thought! Now let's hope there aren't any squeaky floorboards."

Waving a low frequency green night vision LED toward the floor, Rico closely followed Childers through the main level. Both men moved catlike up the stairs and down the hall, padding quietly while spreading out. As he turned a squeaking knob to the end room, Childers was relieved to hear loud snoring. He peeked in and spoke softly into his microphone.

"I've got a positive ID, Skipper. This guy matches the photos you showed us. It's Winston, alright. He's totally out of it, too. I'm ready to move him. Just say the word. There's also no sign of anyone else here."

"No indication of animals either, Captain," Katarina whispered.

"10-4, everyone."

Rico prepared to help grab and scurry off with their target as Childers administered a short spray of tranquilizer below the sleeping target's nostrils. Childers spoke quietly into his radio transceiver: "Just to make sure."

Childers next strapped a wireless monitoring bracelet to gauge the vital signs of their quarry and send the results to Frank Bishop. Moments later, several whiffs were administrated from Childers' black rubber breathing bag for a slightly stronger dose.

"Perfect," Childers told himself. "This guy didn't know what hit him. And the less he remembers about this, the better we all are. Now to get out of here."

Rico stood nearby to help hoist the dozing Winston onto Childers' back. Childers carried Winston down the stairs horsey-style. Ever-vigilant, Childers scanned each window on the way down for signs of any approaching intruders, then spoke into his radio: "Rico, you did your job well—still no unfriendlies detected outside."

Next came the crackle of a radio signal and Rico's whispered response: "Roger that."

Schaefer and Childers retraced their footsteps and were greeted by the stealthy Katarina: "There's nothing going on, Skipper. We've left not a trace here—we are clear."

"Just a minute, everyone," Frank Bishop said over the radio. "I'm not sure what it means, but my street cameras just detected two large vehicles, now parked near the target house. Lights are off, but each has someone in the driver's seat."

Rico spoke next: "Okay, team. Ben, Katarina and I are with the target. We're now reconnoitering for our exit." All of a sudden, light flooded the room. Katarina whipped out her 9mm Heckler & Koch semiautomatic. Spinning on one heel, she pointed her weapon at the offending light source, both arms fully extended. "False alarm, everyone," she whispered. "Must have been an automatic timer. I'll turn it off manually...though I can always use more target practice."

Returning to the pantry, Childers spoke into his transmitter: "Here, Rico. He's all yours. I'll hang back and close up."

Accepting the sliding slumberer from Childers' back, Rico descended into the tunnel with Winston in tow.

"Man, I'm glad I gave up smoking," Rico grunted gratefully. Several minutes later, a crackle in the transmission broke radio silence. "Childers here, Captain. No traces so far. I'm now closing up and ready to re-enter the pantry. Before I lower into the crawlspace, I'll run the glove and bootie check to confirm all are accounted for."

"Good."

A minute later, Childers returned to the airwaves. "Uh-oh."

"Childers, this is Bishop. What do you mean, 'Uh-oh?'"

"I left the bag. The breather bag. It must be on the bed."

"This isn't the time to joke."

"I'm not joking."

Bishop swore under his breath. "Alright, then. Rico will continue hustling our target here to home base. Ben, leave the lid off the crawlspace. Then re-enter the house, grab what you left, get outta there and catch up.

You shouldn't be more than a minute or two behind. Just get *moving*. Katarina, do you read me, too?"

"Yes."

"Good. Just stay where you won't be seen. Katarina, if you aren't in under the house yet, get in there, then wait away from the crawlspace access until Ben joins you."

"Alright," Katarina replied.

Childers returned stealthily to the upstairs bedroom. "Sure enough, Frank. The breathing bag is here on the floor."

Grabbing it, Childers scurried out. He headed back to the crawl space access in the pantry, then watched helplessly as rays from a focused light beam rapidly approached the front door. Suddenly, a bright glare pierced through the front door window curtain, practically blinding him. Ducking down, he kneeled on the floor and held his breath.

"Man, I hope they didn't see me."

On hearing a knock at the door, Childers closed the distance with a running dive into the open pantry and quickly closed the door to the kitchen. In seconds, he jumped down the crawl space, dropped the crawl space cover into place and scurried down the tunnel, practically landing on top of Katarina. Then all hell broke loose. From under the house, it sounded like the front door had blown off.

"Just in time," he whispered. Turning up the light on their miner's hats in unison, the pair hustled. Moments later, a troupe of loud footsteps clattered above them, then faded.

"It sounds like they headed upstairs," Childers whispered to Katarina over his radio microphone, then gently nudged her ahead of him. The two scurried along the tunnel for a few moments, then Katarina stopped.

"Feel this," she whispered anxiously.

"What?"

"Put your hand here and feel this."

"Katarina, I find you very attractive, but really. This is no time..."

"Not that! This! Maybe Rico dropped something. We need to make sure there is nothing left behind."

"Alright," Childers whispered. "Just a second." Childers moved his miner's light toward Katarina while feeling the plastic-encased box she held.

"Look—it's a box. Opening it will make noise and delay us. Just bring it along," Childers said quietly. "Those goons overhead are serious. Let's get moving."

Placing the small container under her arm, Katarina followed Childers. Frightened of betraying their underground location, the team made good time as voices and footsteps became distant. Within a minute, Childers and Katarina had eased through the round tunnel drilled earlier through the earth, leading under one wall of the home's concrete foundation. Next to the tunnel access was a plywood sheet wrapped in black plastic to hamper later detection of the tunnel. "Ingenious," Childers mumbled. "That Schaefer thinks of everything." He slid the plastic covered sheet of plywood into place, providing the team with an added barrier to soundproof the remainder of their exit.

"It's even tighter through here, but my claustrophobia has vanished since we got out from under that house," Childers whispered to Katarina as they crawled on hands and knees. Within minutes, they reached the safe house crawlspace where Schaefer was pushing a comatose Ron Winston up to the main level and into the arms of Rico.

"Rico, now's a good time to shuttle him to our pre-arranged medical facility. Once he wakes up, he should be fine. I'll question him after he comes to."

Childers tapped Schaefer on the shoulder. "Captain. They entered the house. We got out just in time."

"I heard the commotion on my earpiece. What happened?"

"I don't know. But if they smell how close we still are, they might fan out with a team to smoke us out of here."

Wayne Schaefer looked behind Childers. "What do you have there, Katarina?"

"A box. At first I thought we might have dropped it on the way out. But it doesn't look familiar."

"Here. Let me have a look." Grabbing a monstrous serrated SEAL knife from his belt sheath, Schaefer took the package from Katarina in one hand and quickly slit the transparent tape encasing it. He pulled out a film canister from the packet enclosed in a zip-locked plastic bag.

"Well, well," Schaefer intoned. He opened the disk cover, unwound several feet of film and held it up toward the light. "Hmmm. Images of a man and a young kid. Seems kind of familiar. Probably not much to it, but I'll hand it over for forensic review. If anybody can make sense of it, they will."

Repackaging the film, Schaefer lifted himself out of the crawlspace and into the safehouse, before dusting himself off.

"The SUV's are in the garage. Let's give Rico and our 'guest' a head start. Then in a few minutes, the rest of us can all haul out of here." Schaefer looked across the room. "Frank, any chatter on the frequencies you've been monitoring?"

"A bit. It's quiet for now, but about ten minutes ago they requested an investigative unit. Sounds like they think a terrorist 'hit squad' went after their sentries. That's apparently what set them out to enter the target house. The rooftop guys Rico took out weren't responsive, so their team expected the worst."

Schaefer smiled. "Yeah, Frank—once the medication wears off, they're likely to see that they were deliberately unharmed and hopefully calm down a bit. We'll see how long it takes before they suspect CIA involvement. But their risk of media embarrassment ensures they won't go down that road...publicly, at least."

Several hours later, Ron Winston's new environment was a CIA medical facility on the outskirts of Dallas. Winston came to in the post-anesthesia recovery unit with monitoring devices attached all over his body. Interrogating him was Wayne Schaefer.

"What is your name?"

Winston shook his head from side to side. "Ron...Winston."

"What information do you have about the assassination of President John F. Kennedy?"

"What? Who are you?"

"Your activity suggests links to murder. Care to tell us more?"

Winston shifted his bedsheets. "What's this about? And why do you think I have anything to do with murder?"

"Mr. Winston, my name is Wayne Schaefer. I'm a CIA intelligence officer. I'm here to talk with you about any information you have regarding the murder of John Fitzgerald Kennedy. Now, we can do this the easy way, or we can do it the hard way. It's entirely up to you.

But since this involves the murder of a US president, my agency can apply for a provisional change of venue."

Winston took a deep breath. "I am not a terrorist...I'm an American citizen. If you don't believe me, then call my attorney. And if you've been monitoring me, then you'd know his name by now."

"And that would be Mr. Worth?"

"That's right."

"We'll see what we can do."

Several hours later, Dennis Worth entered the room with Winston still in bed.

"Hi Ron," Worth said as he closed the door.

"Dennis. What's happening?"

Worth walked to Winston's bedside. Pulling up a chair, he straddled it backwards and sat down. Looking at his client, he spoke in a hushed tone. "It never gets boring, eh?"

"Dennis, I could use boring right about now."

Worth clasped his hands together across the back of the chair, prayer-like. "Ron, it appears that we're caught up in an inter-agency squabble of sorts."

"Squabble?"

Worth placed an index finger to his lips, motioned to the door with his thumb and continued in a hushed tone. "Ron. Look. At least two federal agencies are fighting over who has custody of you, and by extension, your film."

"Dennis—why should it matter? We're all Americans...and they're both American agencies, to boot."

"Sorry Ron, it's just not that simple."

Worth moved closer to Winston and lowered his voice. "Look. I was going to discuss this with you later...but on my way in here, I finished speaking with representatives from both agencies. Now I see why these two groups have been warring since before the JFK assassination."

"Warring?"

"Basically. A big thing they're maneuvering over is jurisdiction. It's all to better position each organization for damage control, given potentially unflattering revelations that might turn up in the film you have. Like I told you before, one thing to understand about these government people is that they're all about 'pecking order.' And neither agency wants to be the peckee."

"Alright," Winston said, trying to understand as his groggy head absorbed his attorney's analysis.

"Added to their high stakes 'fear of embarrassment,' Ron, is the likelihood of media scrutiny once word gets out about your film. These agencies and their mammoth budgets thrive on predictability, so what concerns them is the unknown...and that could include your film turning into something like the Warren

Commission assassination report and the movie 'JFK,' all rolled into one."

Winston nodded. "I get it...they're all operating out of fear...and 'cover your rear.'"

"Exactly. Like Randall Mackey told us, the JFK assassination is unlike any other criminal mystery in US history. Because it's a crime on American soil, the FBI considers it their turf. Yet, given international intrigue with purported Cuban, Russian and Mob involvement, the CIA sees it differently. Another concern both agencies have is reduced funding for their budgets, particularly if unflattering revelations find their way to the media."

"But where does that leave us, Dennis?"

"Since both agencies want what we've got, in one way we're in a pretty good position. At the moment, we've got some real leverage. If one agency plays tough, all I have to say is that we're still considering releasing the film to the other agency. Then they get reasonable in a hurry."

"Brilliant, Dennis...That's brilliant."

"Thanks, but it's a tad premature for us to congratulate ourselves. Remember, the FBI thinks we have an agreement, even though nothing is signed yet. Anyway, I've arranged another meeting with both groups, but told them both I needed to consult with you first."

"Okay. So what's the bottom line here?"

"If we can get *both* agencies to agree to our terms, and that's a mighty big if...my recommendation would be to consider releasing the film to each agency, simultaneously."

Winston's face grew sour. "What's the advantage to that?"

"A fair question, but actually there are several. One, is that if we go that route, we'd insist on retaining all copyright and public use protections normally afforded the owner of such a film. This can't be overstated, Ron. You need that protection. Second, imagine the media barrage if both the FBI and CIA work their forensics on your film. Information about it is sure to leak out, and the media frenzy to follow will only heighten the exposure—pardon the pun—of your film. That in turn, increases the 'buzz' around it, thereby making it more valuable."

"But valuable to whom?"

"Plenty of people. Organizations, too. Remember, literal fortunes are spent on things like rare art, antique cars, sports cards and baseballs that mark a home run record. The JFK assassination is so much bigger, it's not even close. So let's start with the possibility of our negotiating directly with the government, like perhaps the National Archives. After that, consider wealthy collectors, conspiracy groups, libraries, medical examiner guilds, legal institutions, historical foundations...even foreign interests might make offers for your film. There also appears to be an entire 'conspiracy circuit,' from talk shows to conventions. Yet another possibility would be for us to find a ghost writer for a book deal. We might get something published along the lines of 'I Helped Solve the JFK Assassination Mystery.' You could spend the rest of your life with book signings alone. That is, if you wanted to."

"A book deal? I never would have thought of that one, Dennis."

"Well, in this media age the bottom line is that most publicity is likely to be good. But Ron, there's one other element to consider and that's why I'd like to nail this down sooner, rather than later."

"What's that?"

"If either agency senses they're losing the opportunity for a fair shot, they might simply subpoena you and the film, then throw it all to the courts. If that happens, we could lose everything…particularly if it's deemed a 'national security' concern. These federal agencies have lots of resources and teams of attorneys. They could even join up with other possible claimants, like Sara Maxwell, to wrest the film from you. That's because even though she signed a release, her representatives might claim it was under duress, or that you simply took advantage of an elderly lady and she didn't understand what she was signing. But on top of all that, there's even one more final consideration."

Winston sighed in surrender. "Lay it on me, Dennis."

"By having the expertise of both organizations working on the film, there'll be two separate forensic studies to compare, and hopefully confirm, our findings. If both studies are self-serving to their respective agencies, our guy Randall Mackey has no formal connections to either and he might be seen as the less-biased expert, perhaps a 'tie-breaker,' simply by default. If nothing else, he'll keep both the CIA and FBI honest."

Winston scratched under the monitor on his wrist. "So, Dennis...that's what you suggest as a first step? Speak with each agency and get them to sign a total release on any claim of actual ownership....kind of like a 'quitclaim deed' that we use in real estate?"

"Good analogy."

"Let's do it Dennis. I want to get out of here."

"Consider it done, Ron. I'll talk with Mr. Schaefer and let him know you'll cooperate, to prove you're not a secret agent. That should be enough to get you released once he's satisfied."

"Go get 'em, Dennis."

###

Before sunbreak, Wayne Schaefer hopped into his agency-assigned SUV for the journey to personally brief his old boss on the recent operation. The next day, he pulled into his favorite parking space just before 9:00 AM and smiled upon realizing he'd made the journey in near-record time. Schaefer grabbed a small box under the passenger seat, slammed the car door and marched toward the sprawling CIA complex. Breezing through security checkpoints in short order, he race-walked to the reception desk of his former boss.

"I'm here to see Bailey. He in?"

"Yes—Mr. Bailey just arrived. Was he expecting you?"

"Probably not, but I was to follow up with him. I won't be but a few minutes."

"Please have a seat. I'll let him know you're here."

Schaefer began pouring himself a cup of coffee as Bailey walked in.

"Wayne. Have you been waiting long?"

"Nope. Just got here. Want some coffee?" Schafer said, lifting the coffee pot.

"No thanks, Wayne. Help yourself, though."

"Don't mind if I do, Bailey."

Swiping two chocolate donuts from a neat pile of pastries, Schaefer grabbed a fistful of napkins while balancing his steaming cup of java. He walked into the next room before plopping into a well-padded armchair. Setting his coffee cup on Bailey's desk, Schaefer bit into, then slowly chewed a hunk of the first moist donut.

"Mmmm. These are good!"

Bailey rolled his eyes. "Glad you like them, Wayne. If I'd have known you'd be here, I'd have ordered several dozen." Bailey looked at his watch. "Wayne, I'm not quite sure what you're doing here, unless you've completed your report. Is there a reason why you're not working on a write-up for the mission?"

"Actually, there is. You know I hate paperwork. I figured I'd give it to you in person."

"Well, what is it? How did it go?"

"We have the target and he's talking."

Bailey scooted closer to his desk, clasping his hands together. "Do tell."

"There's not a lot to say for the moment, except the guy seems ready to cut a deal."

"Deal? What kind of a deal?"

"Don't know yet, but it shouldn't be long. His attorney seems pretty eager. Oh, and one other thing," Schaefer said as he placed the small box on his boss's desk. "We found this under the target's house. Do you mind having forensics take a look at it?"

"Sure. What do you think it is?"

"It appears to be movie film. It might be nothing, but given where it was found, I'm guessing it could be more than that."

"I'll be talking with forensics later this morning. I'll hand-deliver it to them."

En route on the drive back to his Dallas area home, Wayne Schaefer saw his phone light up.

"Schaefer here."

"Wayne. This is Dennis Worth. I'm following up with you regarding my client, Ron Winston. I'd like to bring you in on a conference call. At the moment, I have the FBI Director on the line."

"Did you say FBI Director?"

"That's right. I'd like to reach a preliminary meeting of the minds for the moment between the three of us. If you think it sounds workable, we can reduce it to a formal, written agreement on behalf of my client, Mr. Winston."

"I'd have to get final authorization, but I'm fine to hear what you have."

"Okay, that should work. Are you there, Mr. Director?"

"Yes."

"I now have Wayne Schaefer, CIA intelligence officer on the line."

"It appears that this call is encrypted," stated the FBI Director.

"Yes, Mr. Director," said a voice out of nowhere.

"Very well. Go on, then." said the FBI Director.

"My client, Ron Winston, is prepared to simultaneously release the film to both of your agencies, provided we formalize a compact agreeing to protect, defend and indemnify if necessary, his copyright and ownership rights."

There was a long pause. Wayne Schaefer spoke first. "Dennis, I'm pretty sure I can sell that to my supervisor, Louis Bailey and the CIA. One of our primary principles has been to have equal standing with other organizations regarding evidence."

"How about you, Mr. Director?" Dennis replied.

"I'll have to review the document of course, but I believe that could be within the scope of acceptability for the bureau."

"Very well, then. I'll send you each a draft for review by your respective agencies. Once we have a signed agreement, we'll arrange for simultaneous transfer of the film to your respective offices."

###

CIA supervisor Louis Bailey quickly punched numbers on his secure office phone line, then crossed his legs and looked out the window. There was a 'Hello' after two rings.

"Hi Wayne. Bailey here."

"How goes it, old boy?"

"I received a call from the FBI. After reviewing the document from Mr. Winston's attorney, it seems they want to work things out on a fast track."

"Okay," Schaefer said.

"After an inter-agency sit-down, of course."

"Inter-agency sit-down, *of course?*" mocked Schaefer.

"Right," responded Bailey. "The FBI says if we're going to share intel, sooner is best. Otherwise, if media outlets catch wind of this, then make hay out of the rivalry between our agencies, we all lose. Wayne, if you have any concerns about this, let me know. So when you're ready, just give me a call I'll drive you down there."

"Bailey? You're not sitting in with me?"

"Wayne, at that level, even I don't have that high of a clearance. Besides, the only reason you'll be in there is to talk, not listen. Then they'll let you go before the discussion gets really good. You're on a need-to-know basis. At this level, we're talking total compartmentalization. I'll be outside rooting for you, though."

The next day, Schaefer and Bailey were parked at FBI headquarters. "Wayne, I'll be nearby. Call me when it's over and I'll pick you up." With a quick "Wish me luck," Schaefer slammed the passenger side door of Bailey's Mercedes and trudged toward the entry.

"This way please," announced a serious-looking man standing in front of the building. After a short elevator ride, Schaefer was summoned through a long hall, then into a windowless meeting room. Suspended from the ceiling above the table hung a lone omni-directional microphone. As Schaefer walked in, a dozen or so men and women in suits were seated, with a handful of military uniforms on one end. At the other end was a very large video camera. Schaefer was shown to his seat directly in front of it. A gray-haired business-suited man who spoke next was serious, but relaxed.

"Shall we get started? It looks like everyone is here." The gray-haired man smiled. "Thanks everyone, for your punctuality today, because we have a bit to cover. Please bear with me while I go through the security disclosure." The grey-haired man began to read word for word from the document he now held.

"This joint CIA-FBI-DOD hearing hereby convenes to assess soon-to-be released evidence on the John F. Kennedy assassination. We're here for inter-agency deliberation in a spirit of co-operation, using an unprecedented 'team approach.' To ensure maximum confidentiality of this meeting, no note-taking is allowed. By virtue of your attendance at this meeting, each of you hereby swears to uphold the secrecy oath appurtenant to your security clearances, before, during and after this meeting. Please be reminded that records are retained of everyone in attendance. Leaks WILL be traced."

The man put the sheet of paper down. "Okay. That's out of the way. Ladies and gentlemen of the committee. New evidence, in the form of a film, has been uncovered on the JFK assassination. With us today is the man responsible for placing it in the hands of government authorities: CIA intelligence officer Wayne Schaefer. I'll start the ball rolling. Wayne—would you care to describe how this all transpired?"

"Yes, sir," Schaefer responded, shifting in his seat. "I received a call from a family acquaintance around a month ago. A customer in the camera shop he managed asked him to develop the film. As he viewed the film for quality control purposes, my contact noticed the content and called me. From there, I hand-delivered the evidence into the hands of CIA management."

"Thank you, Mr. Schaefer," said the executive-appearing chief. "We've all read your report on securing this new evidence and at this point wanted to first meet you in case there are follow up questions." The executive-appearing chief looked around the meeting table to each person, then focused on the FBI Director. "Mr. Director, in the spirit of co-operation, how committed is the FBI to let go of this old grievance with the CIA?"

"There should be no greater goal than uniting our respective agencies to write the final page of this tragic chapter in our nation's history, together. The Federal Bureau of Investigation will work with our partners in the Central Intelligence Agency and other key agencies like the Department of Defense, to get there, as one team. Armed with what could be key forensic evidence, we look forward to re-doubling our efforts to convict those responsible for the death of our president."

"Very well, then," responded the meeting head. He looked over to a middle-aged man in a dark brown suit. "Can we presume the CIA is prepared to meet the FBI halfway?" Nodding, the man responded "Absolutely. Had I been on board in 1963, we'd have had inter-agency cooperation from the very beginning."

Glancing around the room, the meeting leader smiled. "Thanks again, Mr. Schaefer. Your assistance may help to heal a wound that's been festering for decades. You're dismissed."

Chapter XI

Evidentiary, My Dear Winston

Ron Winston walked down the narrow hallway toward a dimmed viewing room and took his seat next to Dennis Worth. Before them stood forensic photographic expert H. Randall Mackey, appearing scholarly with his bow tie and studious demeanor.

Slicing through the tension, Winston whispered to his attorney: "What, no popcorn?"

Worth smiled. "I didn't see any coming in. Maybe at the intermission."

"They better get popping, then, Dennis. I hear it's a short feature."

The room darkened, falling silent except for a humming laptop. One dim light over Mackey's head provided a halo effect.

"Mr. Winston and Mr. Worth," Mackey nodded toward the two. "I want to thank you for the opportunity to analyze your film. Every job I take on is important, but no project has carried such potential for controversy...or importance to history." Mackey cleared his throat.

"Interesting," Worth commented. "So, what are your results on the film, Randall?"

"Well, I called you both here since the CIA and FBI are each likely reviewing their copies of the film as we speak. To give you both a 'heads up', I felt it was appropriate to provide my preliminary findings, since you might say there appears to be a 'smoking gun.' This way, there'll be few surprises and you can prepare your own case before the court of public opinion as to the meaning and value of the film. My job has been to confirm the veracity from a scientific viewpoint. Needless to say, while the government has unmatched resources, I left no stone unturned and really don't expect the FBI or CIA to detect a whole lot more than what I've noted. But of course, it's always possible." Mackey pushed his eyeglasses high on his nose. "Today you'll be viewing what in fact are now three films."

Winston and Worth looked at each other. "How'd you manage that, Randall?" Worth asked.

"Let me be more specific. There are now three film versions. That's because I first made a duplicate of the film at normal speed, as it was originally processed. In this case, after preserving true copies for safekeeping, we made attempts to lessen the cracked, bleached out portions. Those are common effects of severe heat, particularly around a film's edges. Next, I created an improved enhanced version at normal speed. That's where I 'cleaned it up' using modern film repair technology and digital enhancement techniques. But the version you're about to view now is the third one. This film is enhanced and will be played in slow motion. I'll point to the most significant segments using my laser pointer here as we move through it. If you're ready, let's begin."

Deftly reaching into his pocket to produce a laser pointer, Mackey cleared his throat and calmly announced: "Okay."

As reality hit, Winston felt numb and turned to his attorney. "It all boils down to this, doesn't it, Dennis?"

Worth smiled. "Ron, at some point, we have to know what you've got. Now's as good a time as any."

"It certainly has been long enough."

The room was momentarily dark. Mackey tinkered with his computer as white light suddenly appeared on the screen before them. Mackey pressed a button on his laser pointer. "You're about to view a synchronized, split-screen, frame-by-frame comparison of what we'll call the Winston film, side-by-side next to the Zapruder film."

Ron Winston smiled and looked at his attorney. "Winston film! Did you hear that, Dennis? I'm immortal now."

"Brother."

"While the two films aren't entirely concurrent, I'm able to show the Zapruder film as the Winston film is running," Mackey continued. "That way you have a good idea of where the two cameramen were during key moments of the JFK assassination. In fact, the Winston film appears to have been shot across the street from photographer Abraham Zapruder's perch. This angle offers a unique perspective of both the Texas Schoolbook Depository and also the grassy knoll."

The two side-by-side images each portrayed a dark blue limousine in slow motion. In both films, the president's vehicle was fairly close and approaching. At measured intervals, a new frame appeared for both films. Mackey resumed his play-by-play description.

"What's interesting in this part of the comparison is how the Winston film's perspective of the President's limousine—here on the right—provides a virtually ideal view of the Texas Schoolbook Depository."

The frame-by-frame progression slowed, then halted. Pointing his laser at a close-up frame of the Texas Schoolbook Depository in the Winston film, Mackey chose his words carefully.

"Now notice here on the sixth floor," he cautioned while clicking a small device in his hand. The distant frame zoomed into a close-up of a window. Mackey's laser pointer circled around an object protruding from the structure.

"Dennis and Ron. What does…THIS…look like to you?"

Worth spoke first. "It's kind of hard to tell."

"Yeah, it is kind of grainy," Ron added.

"Okay. Fair enough. How about if I improve the contrast. Then add a little more hue for some color and sharpen the focus?"

Seconds later, Worth and Winston gasped in unison.

Mackey took a step back and crossed his arms. "That's what I thought, too. Let's pause here." He turned off the computer. "Lights, please. I'll hand out a printed version of what you just saw and show you what I think we're dealing with." Mackey handed 8x10 glossies to Winston and Worth. "Look very closely at the image I've circled in the window of the Texas Schoolbook Depository. That circle shows where alleged JFK assassin Lee Harvey Oswald had his sniper's perch. Now...draw your eye four windows to the left."

"It looks like either a fishing pole, a boom microphone, a shotgun or a rifle," exclaimed Worth.

"Exactly. Which puts a prospective second shooter in another area of the Texas Schoolbook Depository. This provides a vantage point similar to what Lee Harvey Oswald would have had. It also offers a good 'back up' in case one of the two shooters either gets caught, waylaid or cold feet. But hold your breath...there's more," Mackey declared as he pulled another 8x10 glossy from his folder before pointing at it.

"The person who shot the Winston film was moving around a lot. However, the big 'plus' there is that it gives us more than a single perspective. Because the cameraman pointed his movie lens almost wildly in different places throughout the assassination, it allows us to view several disparate areas of the murder scene, not just the Texas Schoolbook Depository, all within a short time spam. To enhance the Winston film to the highest degree, the trick was to wait for a clear frame, then enlarge it. What I'm about to show you is another video-capture from one of the later clearest images in the

Winston film. After quite a bit of enlarging, I was able to focus on the one image I'd consider a 'smoking gun' if ever there was one."

Winston brought the photo close to his face and pointed. "A smoking gun barrel," he breathed.

"That looks like it's from behind the white fence on the grassy knoll," Worth exclaimed.

"Correct," Mackey agreed. "But short of corroborating forensics, at this point we're not able to ascertain who these apparent shooters are, or the entities they represent. For that, we'll be better served by having the CIA and FBI work it out. Given their near-unlimited resources, that should give them both a terrific hand-up."

"And if they don't?" Winston queried.

"Then no amount of evidence will ever make a difference." Mackey continued. "I'm no conspiracy theorist, but these images either point them in the right direction, or something's gravely amiss. That's because there's really only one entity with access to most of the facts."

Mackey sighed, then resumed with a knowing smile. "After all, who interviewed witnesses after the assassination? The US government," Mackey answered himself rhetorically. "And who spent millions on the Warren Commission Report to ascertain the truth? The US government." Mackey stopped for a moment, then continued. "Who will have this new information and the forensic know-how to wring every last drop of evidence to find the perpetrators? The US government. And who had certain records on the Kennedy assassination sealed for decades?"

Winston and Worth replied in unison. "The US government."

"Right. So on the plus side, if the US government wants to ultimately find President Kennedy's killer, they now have more evidence to do so. The only problem," Mackey continued, "is that if some inside the US government are at all complicit in burying this intel, given that certain Kennedy assassination files were long sealed."

"Then they may not want to follow where this new evidence leads," Worth responded.

Mackey shook his head. "Exactly. Let's just hope any publicity about this will force government officials to re-open the investigation and get the job done right this time."

As the doorbell rang, Ron Winston looked up from his morning newspaper and coffee.

"Who's that this early?" he mumbled. With a loud "Just a minute," Winston walked to his front door. Opening it, he was greeted by two dour-looking men dressed in business casual attire. Each wore a dark blue blazer, khakis and dark sunglasses. Both were in their mid-thirties. The black-haired man was clearly in charge. He spoke firmly and upon removing his sunglasses, Winston noticed a scar below one eye.

"Ron Winston?"

"That's me. Who wants to know?"

"Mind if we come in? Government business."

"Uh, can I see some ID or something?"

"Certainly."

Each man whipped out a leather wallet with photo ID stamped 'FBI.' Winston looked at his visitors incredulously.

"FBI? Hey, my attorney has already talked with you."

Looking over his shoulder, the lead man resumed speaking. "You're not in any trouble."

Winston relaxed.

"Is anyone else in the house?"

"Uh, no. I live alone."

"May we come in?"

"Since you're asking, fine." Turning, Winston shrugged his shoulders. The two followed behind, almost crowding him. The three retreated to the peaceful atmosphere of Winston's carpeted living room, his large aquarium fish tank softly buzzing in the background. Winston gestured at a sofa.

"Go ahead and have a seat."

"Thank you."

"So—government business, huh? Mind telling me what it's about?"

"Mr. Winston, we're here to debrief you."

"Shouldn't my attorney be here?"

"If you insist. However, it's faster without a third party. In the interest of federal disclosure, we're simply here to inform you that along with providing protective services to you recently, we've also been observing your activities over the past few weeks."

"Why? I'm not the bad guy in all this."

"Decision makers—all the way to the top—agreed this was the rarest of opportunities."

"What do you mean?"

"We knew you possessed possible evidence on the JFK assassination. As a result, we searched your house under court order to confirm that fact."

"Searched my house? What did you find?"

"Nothing relating to our investigation."

"Couldn't you have just called my attorney?"

"We prefer to work that way. But since circumstances involved a presidential murder, the justice department agreed we were perfectly within the limits of the law. Fact is, they consider the JFK assassination as more of a terrorist act and not only murder."

Winston looked back and forth at both men.

"Guys, I wasn't the criminal here."

The quiet one spoke next. "Believe us, we'd like to take every citizen at their word. But understand, without regard to guilt or innocence, the theory works this way: Any party with a hand in the murder of President Kennedy would go to extreme lengths— certainly murder—to lay hands on, and then destroy evidence of their own involvement. So when we received word of potential new evidence, we immediately began monitoring you with GPS positioning, along with a variety of other surveillance techniques. Actually, you might even consider thanking us. That's because during the course of our surveillance, we prevented several attempts on your life before they got too close."

Winston shook his head. "So I was bait."

The lead man recited his spiel coolly. "Given the round-the-clock protection you received during our surveillance, we'd prefer not to think of it that way. In a very real manner, let's just say you did your country a great service. As a result, we now have a dossier on multiple international crime syndicates who appear to have targeted you—each with a link to the assassination."

"So you knew my life has been in danger?"

The lead agent spoke in a monotone. "We had little choice."

A light bulb flashed in Winston's head. "Did your guys take out that hit team gunning for me in the alley?"

Both men slowly shook their heads.

"We can't go into detail, but let's just say you were covered from the moment we learned of the film. And it worked."

"Worked?"

"As a consequence, we are now holding—at an undisclosed location—agents of Cuban intelligence."

"So the Cubans killed President Kennedy and were after me to squelch the film?"

"It's not quite that simple."

"What do you mean?"

"We're also holding several agents of the former KGB."

"Teamwork, eh? They were in it together, I'll bet."

The quiet agent said nothing as the lead man continued. "It's just not as tidy as you might think."

Winston's eyes lit up in amazement. "There's more?"

"Without going into great detail, we're also holding members of a well-known New York crime family."

Winston's mind raced. "That makes sense. Foreign governments put our mob up to it, to make it look like an 'inside' job."

"Sorry to correct you."

"More?"

"Something like that. We're also researching prospective rogue elements of the CIA, FBI, Secret Service and key US military personnel."

Winston laughed. "So who actually *is* responsible for the president's murder?"

"We can't discuss a pending case until after each suspect's statements are scrutinized and evidence reviewed. Remember—it has taken decades since the JFK assassination for us to get this far. It'll take a rather arduous series of interrogations over a period of months, even years, to sort this out."

"I can't figure out why you're even here, telling me all this. What do you want from me?"

The two agents shared glances. Then the quiet man talked. "As we work together with the CIA, we realize you will be given media opportunities. Both our agencies would appreciate an understanding that nothing be revealed to the press without government review."

"Why's that?"

"We'd prefer that others currently under surveillance not be given a 'heads up,' unless required by court order."

"I'm afraid you guys are a little late."

"Late? What do you mean?"

"Here. I recorded it." Winston walked over to the television and hit a switch to play the latest news. On the screen, Dennis Worth stood before the podium, sweat already beading on his forehead from the countless klieg lights arranged for news cameras. He cleared his throat and began to read from his prepared text.

"Ladies and gentlemen of the press. Thank you for being here on this historic day. After decades of controversy, it's our hope the final chapter to President Kennedy's assassination is in the process of being written. Before I get started, though, I must stress this is only as the result of much team-work. But let me start by introducing myself, because you may be wondering who I am. I'm Dennis Worth, here to represent my client, Mr. Ron Winston."

"Spell your names please," shouted a voice from the crowd. Worth smiled.

"My last name is spelled W-o-r-t-h and my client is Ron Winston, last name spelled W-i-n-s-t-o-n."

A reporter stood up. "Mr. Worth, do your findings indicate who killed President Kennedy?"

Worth looked out at the cameras and took a noticeably deep breath. "For that, I'd like to introduce Mr. Mackey, our forensics team leader. Randall?"

Mackey stood up and strolled to the podium, then took a quick sip from a bottle of water. "Thank you, Dennis. Ladies and gentlemen, thank you for your patience in what has become our nation's longest nightmare. You've probably never heard of me before, but I'm Randall Mackey, a forensic photographic specialist."

"Please spell your name," yelled a voice from the crowd.

"Sure. R-a-n-d-a-l-l...M-a-c-k-e-y. The bottom line of our investigation appears to support a second gunman...even possibly a third gunman."

The crowd murmured for a few moments, then quieted down, before a reporter stood.

"With all due respect, Mr....uh, Mackey...There have been plenty of discounted experts who've weighed in on the Kennedy assassination. Where were these alleged gunmen seen on the film you viewed and why are your insights any different or more relevant than all the others we've already heard?"

Mackey rubbed the back of his neck and shook his head briefly. "That's a great question and actually, while my research is well-documented, you shouldn't trust me any more than anyone else. I'm simply here to say that our findings support the presence of at least two gunmen in addition to Texas Schoolbook Depository shooter Lee Harvey Oswald. I can also explain why that is consistent with photographic evidence already seen by millions of Americans, the Zapruder film. But let's start with the facts."

Mackey took a swig of water before continuing. "Given the ballistic evidence, multiple wounds and myriad problems with the 'magic bullet' theory, there has long been support for at least a second shooter. In addition, Mr. Oswald's weapon of choice on that fateful day was a Mannlicher-Carcano rifle, not known for remarkable accuracy—even in the hands of an expert. Plus, our evidence of a second gunman places him near Oswald in the Texas Schoolbook Depository building. This would have provided the killers added firepower from high up without adding significant risk of being discovered…that is, unless a camera happened to have recorded that second rifle, which we believe is the case."

Another reporter stood. "What's the story on a suspected *third* gunman?"

"While less corroborative, the presence of a third gunman cannot be discounted and for several very good reasons. First, our findings put the suggested location of this potentially third gunman precisely where witnesses have long placed him…on the grassy knoll. If you look at photos from that day in Dealey Plaza, many observers pointed in that direction after the shooting. Second, a gunman located from the area of the grassy knoll helps explain some of the president's injuries, particularly the one which wounded him mortally."

###

A late night knock on his door interrupted Wayne Schaefer's bedtime reading. Schaefer was trained to assume all late night door visitors were suspect. At 11:30 PM, he was in no mood to deal with a lost neighborhood drunk, a local punk—or worse. Opening the nightstand drawer, he grabbed an unloaded .357 magnum revolver. Yanking on the cylinder release, he shoved his paw between the mattress and extracted a circle of bullets encapsulated within a handgun auto-feeder. "Who is it?" Schaefer snarled over his shoulder at the door. Rapidly filling the weapon, he snapped the cylinder shut with one circular action.

"It's me, Mr. Schaefer."

The voice was familiar. Schaefer mouthed the response and began to think. "Mr. Schaefer? Must be a kid. Didn't I pay my newspaper delivery boy already this month?" Growing curious, but alert for a ruse, Schaefer padded down the hallway to his front door, gun in hand. "Just a minute."

Peeking through the peephole, he had a hard time believing what he saw. "Well, I'll be," he announced. Schaefer slid the revolver into the pocket of his bathrobe and threw open the door.

"Skip Hollister! What are you doing here?"

"I hope it isn't too late to stop by, Mr. Schaefer."

269

"Not at all, Skip," Schaefer said, shaking the young man's hand. Come on in—it's getting cold."

As Hollister entered the house, Schaefer motioned the young man to a chair. "Can I get you something to drink or eat?"

"Oh, no—I'm fine, thanks."

Schaefer furrowed his brow. "Everything alright?"

"Great, Mr. Schaefer."

"What brings you to the neighborhood?"

"My old employer is closing down. With everyone developing their own film anymore, there just isn't enough business."

Hollister nervously cleared his throat. "Mr. Schaefer, I've been thinking about what you said a few months ago…"

"Yes? About what?"

"That the new CIA is different than the one my Dad and you worked for."

"That's right," Schaefer responded. "It *is* different. Standards are high, so it's tough to get in now. But conditions, especially for young people like you, are a whole lot better."

"Do you think you could help me get an interview?"

Schaefer smiled. "Why, sure. I can do better than that."

Hollister looked curious. "Really? How?"

"Before any interview, I'll get you a great reference letter. Coming from an experienced hand like me, it shouldn't hurt."

The next morning after an uneventful flight out of Dallas, Schaefer smiled as he arrived in the parking lot of his old boss. Rushing through security, he headed straight for Bailey's office. Schaefer breezed through the waiting room and past the receptionist with minimal comment. "I'm here to see Bailey." Entering the office, Schaefer was greeted with a knowing smile.

"Wayne!"

"Hey, Bailey. You get the news?"

"Get the news? I'm just now in the process of shopping for your Cuban cigars to present."

Bailey looked down and began tapping his watch. "Best of all, Wayne...instead of using up all your allotted time, by my calculations you completed the job with one hour and twenty minutes to spare."

Schaefer rolled his eyes. "Not like you were keeping track, or anything."

"Wayne, you and your team pulled this one off just like you said you would. I knew it all along. Have a seat." Bailey's phone intercom beeped.

"Mr. Bailey, there's a call for you on the green line."

"The green line? Do you know who it is?"

"They said it's from the office of the president." Bailey and Schaefer smiled at one another. "Well, put him on," Bailey said while activating the phone speaker. "We can't keep him waiting."

"White House phone exchange. The president will speak with you now."

"Yes, this is Louis Bailey."

"Hello and good morning, Mr. Bailey."

"Good morning, Mr. President. I'm here with case officer Wayne Schaefer."

"It's an honor to speak with you, Mr. President," Schaefer said.

"It's good to speak with you both. On my desk this morning, I received a briefing of your work. I understand you've tenaciously pursued evidence on one of our country's toughest cases. On behalf of the American people, I want to thank you and your team for helping unite the FBI and CIA so they can finally solve this case."

Bailey blushed before responding. "Why thank you, Mr. President. I can't take credit. But case officer Wayne Schaefer, can." Schaefer turned red.

"Wayne and Louis, on behalf of a grateful nation, I thank you both. Because of your hard work, our country may soon be able to finally put this sad chapter behind us for all time. As a token of appreciation, I'm inviting you both to a gala event coming up in a few months and hope both your families will attend. My office will coordinate it. Again, thank you both and God bless America."

Schaefer and Bailey replied in unison: "God bless America."

Hanging up the telephone, the president looked over to the director of the United States Secret Service. "By working together instead of against each other, the CIA and FBI are finally getting close to figuring the JFK assassination out, aren't they?"

The Secret Service director smiled. "Let's just say they're getting in over their heads…and if they're not careful, they're about to go under."

www.11-22-1963.com

CPSIA information can be obtained
at www.ICGtesting.com
Printed in the USA
LVOW10s0131170717
541577LV00017B/1345/P